FLIGHT OF THE STAR DRAGON

AN EARTH FORCE SKY PATROL FILE: SOLAR YEAR 2387

BLAZE WARD

KNOTTED ROAD PRESS

Flight of the Star Dragon
An Earth Force Sky Patrol File: Solar Year 2387
Blaze Ward
Copyright © 2019 Blaze Ward
All rights reserved
Published by Knotted Road Press
www.KnottedRoadPress.com

ISBN: 978-1-64470-050-1

Cover art:
ID 8852268 © diversepixel | DepositPhoto.com

Cover and interior design copyright © 2019 Knotted Road Press

Never miss a release!
If you'd like to be notified of new releases, sign up for my newsletter.

I will never spam you, or use your email for nefarious purposes. You can also unsubscribe at any time.

http://www.blazeward.com/newsletter/

The Jessica Keller Chronicles

Auberon

Queen of the Pirates

Last of the Immortals

Goddess of War

Flight of the Blackbird

The Red Admiral

St. Legier

Winterhome

CS-405

Queen Anne's Revenge

Packmule

Persephone

Additional Alexandria Station Stories

The Story Road

Siren

Two Bottles of Wine with a War God

The Science Officer Series

The Science Officer

The Mind Field

Imposters

VANIR

IT HAD BEEN a month since Gareth's transformation. A month of looking at a new face in the mirror in the morning.

Talyarkinash had printed a picture for him, a photo taken back when he was still human. He had grown into his Vanir face, but it was still damnably odd, comparing the man he had become with the man he had been as recently as six weeks ago.

The ears were probably the hardest part to adjust to. On a human, they were rounder, both on the top and the bottom. His new Vanir ears were almost pointed at the top, like cartoon depictions of elves. Sleeker. Taller too, by maybe a whole inch.

Gareth couldn't tell if it was new ears that had made his hearing any sharper, or all the other modifications that had come with what Talyarkinash had done to him, with the help of the two Yuudixtl scientists: Morty and Xiomber.

Similarly, his eyes were ever-so-much bigger as a

fraction of his face. And wider, coming out to sharper corners that almost made him feel half-Japanese, if there was such a thing. Cheekbones had grown more angular, sharper planes than his more-rounded face and head had been.

At least the soft, blond beard covered part of his face, and blurred some of the changes. It had finally grown in enough that it stopped itching, but it still threw him off when he saw that person in the mirror.

It was Gareth St. John Dankworth. Field Agent of Earth Force Sky Patrol, Missile Division, 6th Cavalry Troop. Except it wasn't, anymore.

Probably never would be again, unless something magical happened.

More magical.

More bizarre than all the things that he had seen since Morty and Xiomber pulled him through an illegal wormhole from Earth Force's base in the Earth/Moon L2, *The Arsenal*. Dragged him into the wider galaxy. To the *Accord of Souls*, which humans could also never become members of.

But he was still a cop. A protector of the innocent. He would do that here, as long and as well as they allowed him.

Gareth wiped both hands down his face, watching the stranger in the mirror do the same. He ran his hands back though blond hair that should have been cut six weeks ago. At this point, he was likely to turn into a bohemian, a surfer pretty soon, with long, curly locks already touching his collar and perhaps down to his shoulder blades in another year.

A Field Agent would never be that far outside of

regulations, unless he was a Secret Agent operating under cover. But Gareth wasn't a Field Agent these days. Might never be again.

Would most likely never see Earth again. Or his friends. His family.

Or Pippa.

Gareth reached into a pocket of his pants and pulled out the tiny, leather pouch his still kept with him at all times. From inside, he pulled out the gold ring with the single, white diamond in the middle, surrounded by ruby and gold stones representing Sky Patrol.

Today, they represented *Loss*. The life he could never go back to. The sacrifices he had been called upon to make, in the name of duty.

He had considered asking Talyarkinash to find a way to clone his body and turn it back into the human he had been, so that they could return it to Earth and he could be declared formally dead. Pippa might wait the rest of her life for a man who could never return. And even if he did, she was still human, so they could never have children. Never be a family.

He tucked the ring and the pouch back into his pocket and sighed heavily.

Never *be*.

Gareth emerged from the small bathroom into his suite. It was as identical to his cabin, back at the Arsenal, as he had been able to make it, both in layout and content. A single bed, or whatever the equivalent was when he was seven-feet-four-inches tall and had a seventy-inch chest. The chester had been scaled up as well, but still had four drawers, white paint, and a flat top. A reading chair by the bathroom, warm and comfortable. A table and two chairs by the door.

Home. Or a reasonable imitation thereof.

He grabbed his tunic from where he had dropped it on the bed and pulled it on. Constabulary Blue, like his pants. Almost the color of his blue-gray eyes. So tight as to be a second skin, but somehow woven with a layer of triangular scales covering much of the exterior and providing protection against blunt and edged weapons.

The uniform of a Constable. Or whatever Gareth was. He hadn't been to their police school, but had come back to his cabin after dinner every night and studied and read everything he was allowed access to. Back home, he had been a Field Agent of Sky Patrol, so he knew how to be a cop.

Here, he was introduced to anyone who visited this facility as an Explorer, roughly equivalent to a Patrolman, or a Deputy Agent back home. It was a good enough cover story. The fewer people that knew the truth, the safer everyone would be.

He had no idea what the actual truth was either.

Gareth turned and found the digital clock sitting on the chester, counting slowly. Getting used to a twenty-eight-hour day had been possibly the smallest thing, as well as the weirdest, in a month of complete nonsense.

Fourteen meant local zenith. Back home, time for lunch. Here, breakfast was at six, lunch was at eleven, dinner was at sixteen, and supper was at twenty-one. Four meals, instead of the three he grew up with, but Gareth just pretended that third meal was the equivalent of English High Tea and that all sort of made it all work in his head.

Dr. Royston Loughty, PhD, FRS, CBE, CStJ, and Pippa's father, would have called it a serious case of culture shock, and he would have been correct. But there wasn't anything Gareth could do but roll forward and figure it all out as he went.

That was all any of them could do, but their lives hadn't been nearly as upended as his.

Gareth held his elbows out and flexed, making sure his tunic stretched right. According to Talyarkinash, it would move with him when he changed forms, becoming somehow absorbed into his flesh when he did, and adding an extra layer of dermal armor when…

How did you explain it to a complete stranger that had never seen it happen? That Gareth St. John Dankworth, as a human, did not have any of the limitations to his genetics that the Chaa, the **Elders** who had uplifted all of the species of the *Accord of Souls* and then bound them into a psionic unity, had put on all the others.

What vocabulary did you use to explain that you could turn into a thing he called a Star Dragon?

Gareth shrugged and headed towards the door of his cabin. He didn't want to be late to his meeting. Constable Baker and Senior Constable Grodray would be there.

Gareth hoped that meant that there would be action soon.

CONSTABLE

EVETH BAKER CONSIDERED the view as the vehicle cruised through the late-morning sky of *Irron*. It wasn't an auto-taxi, but a similar vehicle, privately owned by the Constabulary to transport officers around. The craft was low and sleek, done in the Constabulary's traditional steel blue inside and out, with a comfortable cabin that would seat eight Vanir or a dozen Grace on the two benches running parallel to the sides. She and Grodray had the plush, warm seats to themselves.

According to her partner, Jackeith Grodray, the blue overhead was among the closest to the planet *Earth* where Dankworth had been born and lived his whole life. Hopefully, that had helped with his acclimation.

She didn't like it, any of it, but they were going to need his help.

The sky was clear and a blue that just seemed artificial to her eyes, but she was used to more urban places like *Orgoth Vortai* or *Hurquar*. *Irron* was almost a nature preserve, by comparison, with few cities of any note and vast wilderness areas covering much of the planet still.

The Constabulary maintained one of their largest training facilities out here, away from civilian eyes that might not react well to loud noises and activities of the men and women training to protect the many worlds of the *Accord of Souls*.

Below, a plateau stretched out, overlooking a gorge that seemed bottomless in the fog and spray of a tremendous river waterfalling over one thousand meters into a lake so blue it might have been tanzanite.

"Kopek for your thoughts, Eve?" her partner asked, looking up from his digital book as the cruiser banked and started its descent to the base revealed below them in the trees.

"You'd get overcharged, Jack," she said. "Still not sure what we're doing here. What I'm doing here. What the hell happens next. You know?"

"You're here because you impressed the hell out of my bosses and helped break open a major smuggling and genetics operation, Baker," the man turned serious. "Lot of sunlight suddenly shining in on places where it never should have left. We'll be years cleaning up all the corruption revealed. This might be one of the biggest cases in our lifetimes."

Eveth shrugged. She was a cop. That was why she had joined in the first place. Stopping bad guys.

"And Dankworth?" she turned to face him. The ground was rushing up to meet them, but she had been here before, and this runway wasn't all the impressive, once you had already flown next to the waterfall overlooking a kilometer drop.

"He's here because he has nowhere else to go," Grodray nodded once. Sharp. Fierce. Decisive. "He's a cop, like us, trying to save the galaxy. And everybody is still trying to identify a way we can stop Maximus without him, but nobody's come up with anything better."

"He's a monster, Grodray," she snapped.

"We're all monsters, Baker," he replied in that cold, flat voice he got when he was past teasing. "Sane people do not take up arms and put on a badge. They become musicians. Or shopkeepers. Something predictable. That's why Kathra divorced me and remarried. Too many nights alone when the kids were young. It's why she found a second husband who's a sales manager. Safe. Quiet. Comfortable. But someone has to do this job. Someone has to hold the line against all the people trying to cheat the system and make an unfair profit. Without the *Accord*, you have chaos."

"Or Maximus," she mused, mostly to herself, but apparently loud enough for him to hear.

"Or something worse, yes," Grodray acknowledged. "I remember Maximus telling Gareth about his plan to become Emperor Marc the First, an immortal human who was planning to take over the entire *Accord* with the help of more humans, and rule forever."

"So we have to trust another human to save us?"

she sneered. It wasn't meant to come out that bitter, but even she heard the tones in her voice.

So did Grodray. His eyes got hard.

"That man has sacrificed everything, Eve," Jackeith's voice dropped to a murmur. "Everything. And I've not heard any reports of him complaining about it afterwards. He's lost his past, his present, and his future. All his friends and family. The woman he loved. And he would do it again tomorrow, if we asked. Keep that in mind."

"I know, Grodray," her own voice dropped as the cruiser landed lightly. "Will it be enough?"

"I don't know, Eve," he said. "But we've got to try."

CRIME BOSS

IT HAD BEEN a month from hell. Marc had no other way to quantify it. Six weeks ago, he had been the functional ruler of the entire world of *Zathus*, living in the shadows yes, but with his tentacles into almost every aspect of that world's economy and polity.

Granted, he had inherited most of that power from that idiot Warreth, the birdman Cinnra, but the gang Marc had taken control of, the small army of corrupt officials and merchants, did his bidding. Nobody did anything major without a nod or a word.

And then those two lizardmen had turned on him and ruined everything.

Even Marc had been shocked at how tenuous his organization had turned out to be, so maybe it had been for the best that it had all gone down the way it had. He had shut down the main facility on *Zathus* and sent everyone into hiding before going to *Hurquar*, bringing on twenty-five people with him.

Of those, ten had made it out of the trap that he had managed to spring on himself.

Even Marc wasn't so arrogant as to suggest it was anybody's fault but his own. He could have killed Gareth instead of taking him prisoner. But he had wanted information that the Nari woman had. And the two Yuudixtl. They had been the ones that had upgraded Marc in the first place, taking a lowly human and turning him into something even more dangerous.

Seven-foot-four. Three hundred and forty pounds of muscle. Genius-level intellect to go with it.

And he was still human, underneath. At least in all the ways that mattered. Everyone else belonged to the *Accord of Souls*. Psionically linked to one another in such a way that intramural violence was almost impossible.

Almost.

There were a few. There were always a few who slid into the cracks. Criminals born wrong, to hear the locals talk. As if that was a mental-health issue that could be fixed with a little genetic surgery. Just undo those miswired neurons and you'd be right as rain.

And boringly obedient.

Humans didn't have those limits. Marc Sarzynski wore the physical form of a Vanir, but his soul was still human. Some of his old gang have lived in fear of that. Many of them had turned on him.

Like this stupid bastard.

Marc looked down on the Elohynn tied to the chair with cruelly-tight leather straps. They were in a warehouse, another in an immeasurable string of them, where Marc and his closest associates had hidden like rats when the Constabulary had suddenly known too much about too many things.

Like perhaps someone had started feeding them tidbits, not realizing that he was the only person who knew some of them, so things could be traced back to him.

The room was cold, but Marc was sweating with effort. He had stripped down to dungarees and a T-shirt with some band he had never heard of on the front.

The Elohynn was sweating, too.

They were alone in this office. Several of Marc's people were outside, where they could watch though the big picture window if they wanted, but he doubted most of them had the stomach for it. Maiair and Yooyar probably, the Warreth sisters who were fast becoming his indispensable right and left hands. Zorge, the Nari physicist-turned-spymaster. They had been there when Gareth Dankworth had unleashed his ultimate abomination on the galaxy.

When he had transformed into a dragon.

Damabiath the Elohynn had obviously thought that he could get away with it. Too many raids had gotten too close. Maybe the Elohynn planned to make a little profit feeding the cops tips about Marc's whereabouts for the reward money. Something. It had worked.

Right up until he forgot that he was dealing with a Vanir that had a 200 IQ and absolutely no qualms about doing violence to one of his fellow sentient creatures.

Marc missed his medical theater equipment. It had been perfect for slowly torturing his enemies into revealing the little tidbits that he had needed to take control of the gang, and the underworld, and eventually the cops and prosecutors on *Zathus*.

But he didn't want anything from Damabiath.

Well, technically that wasn't true. There was just nothing that the Elohynn could tell Marc that he didn't already know. Or wanted to know.

No, they had a much more personal conclusion, and it was at hand.

The Elohynn was naked. Marc understood the importance of removing the clothes from a victim. The psychological effects of being completely unmasked.

This particular species tended to run taller than humans, perhaps six and a quarter to six and a half feet for the men. The slightest bit smaller for the women. Plus those gorgeous wings.

Mark Sarzynski was a head taller now.

The angelic criminal was seated, which just emphasized the size difference. The straps holding his arms and legs to the chair were too tight, cutting off circulation in ways that would start to be troublesome in another hour or so.

If it mattered.

His wings were stretched out as far as they would go sideways, and then held in place by spikes Marc had personally punched into the tips and attached to chains in the walls, far enough back that Damabiath couldn't pull them loose by tearing skin. Not without breaking bones first.

The man's mouth was gagged with a piece of leather that showed intense bite marks, but had resisted all attempts for the Elohynn to get through it. Maybe if he had a few more hours he could have managed.

Marc reached down and picked up a pair of pliers. They were already covered with blood and down at this point, so he wiped them slowly on a messy towel that had been clean a hour ago.

Marc examined his victim closer. All the feathers had been individually plucked from the left wing. From his studies, that was the single most debilitating fear any Elohynn could face. Many chose self-termination, rather than lose the ability to fly and be relegated to the "two-dimensional crowd," as they tended to view the rest of the *Accord*.

Marc watched the eyes follow the pliers, rather than the wielder. There didn't appear to be any mind left inside there at this point. Marc hadn't asked a single question once he got the man trussed up like a turkey for the plucking.

Just pain. Artfully applied, as if a psychotic Grace had needed to create a new sculpture installation.

Idly, Marc wondered if he might locate a Grace who viewed such torture as art. With their sensory tentacles, they might be perfect for this sort of thing if he could break their operant conditioning hard enough. Elohynn, conversely, were among the most empathic species in the *Accord*, so they could never really abide with pain, unless they were so crazy as to be dangerous. It made them good counsellors, and reasonable bankers, but lousy criminals.

Slowly, Marc replaced the pliers on the bench and picked up a knife. Damabiath had betrayed him. Sold him to the Constabulary for thirty pieces of silver and the hopes for a pardon. Expected that he would never be identified. Wouldn't have, but for an inside leak, a data clerk with a gambling problem, trying to reduce her debt with information for Maximus.

"And now, we have reached the final stage of our conversation," Marc said in a low tone.

Damabiath tried to say something through the gag. Tried to scream, perhaps, with what little was left of his mind and his soul.

"You, of all people, should have known how I deal with traitors, Damabiath," Marc scolded the man. "You were there. You watched the punishment. Helped even, by providing me the proof I needed to unearth one of the conspiracies against me. My, how the mighty have fallen."

Marc considered the being. His eyes were all whites at this point, painting a masterpiece in red blood and sweating skin.

"I do not feel good about this," Marc admitted quietly. "Any of it. But you people have forgotten that I'm not one of you. Am not bound by your ridiculous morality. And even then, I probably wouldn't have been reduced to something so petty as this, but someone had to become an example. The children of the night need to fear me more than they do the Constabulary. In that, your life will provide one, last, valuable lesson."

Marc stepped forward and slammed the blade into the Elohynn's chest with all his augmented might, driving it straight through the fragile keel bone and cutting his heart in two. There was precious little blood, and the light went out of the man's eyes quickly.

Marc pulled the knife from the cooling corpse, cleaned it, and set it with the other tools, taking the time to methodically pack things away. Hopefully, this would send the correct message and he would never have to do this again.

How in the nine hells had Marc Sarzynski, Deputy Agent of Earth Force Sky Patrol, fallen so far? He considered all the tiny steps that brought him thus. None of them included a concrete commitment to evil.

And yet, here he was.

This road wasn't even paved with good intentions. No. Easy clips. Corners cut. Mistakes when he tried to finally come out ahead of Gareth St. John Dankworth once and for all, only to fall ever so short, time and again.

And worse, he knew in his soul Dankworth hadn't been competing. Or rather, not with Marc. Gareth had been competing with himself to become the best agent he could imagine.

Marc's jealousy at second place was just a terrible taskmaster.

The door opened and closed, noisily enough as to be obvious. Marc glanced up. Maiair, her red crest at half-mast. Powerful, but not threatening. Supportive.

He would make her a queen, once he had regained his power. Not an Empress, but close. He would need her and her sister, and there was no better way to bind them to his throne.

"The body?" she asked simply, standing more or less at attention, but turned in such a way that she didn't have to see or acknowledge the mess. Yooyar and Zorge waited outside the office, still visible through glass, but separated by the closed door.

Middle managers, as it were.

Marc considered his options. Terror was an effective tool, but it must be used like the edge of a razor, slicing a little at a time and withdrawing. Overuse would render it comically less effective. People could become inured to such atrocities if they became commonplace.

Once should hold everyone in fear for a year or more.

"Leave him," Marc said in a heavy voice.

It was acceptable for Maiair to know that he took no pleasure in this task. No pride in a well-tortured opponent. That he still had his humanity, underneath it all.

"After we have made it to safety, contact a journalist," he decided. "Give them the address and leave the door unlocked. Damabiath on the evening news will send the message to anyone wavering at this point."

"Won't the Constables know it was us?" she pressed.

"They already know we're on this planet," Marc said. "I need the local underworld to hide me. They must fear me more than they do that damnable dragon."

"Understood," she said as she turned. She hesitated.

"What?" Marc snapped, as he faced her.

"Are you all right?" she asked in a quiet voice. Nervous about overstepping an undrawn boundary.

"If I never have to do that again, it will still be too soon," he replied. "But this has become a war. And bad things are likely to happen."

SCIENTIST

"ARE you sure this is the sort of place you wish to go, father?" Pippa asked Royston as they approached the front door of the concert hall, surrounded by youngsters, teenagers frequently flirting with hooliganism but still safely on this side of the line.

Royston nodded, watching the scene with his pursed lips set in a firm, disapproving line.

There was no choice. Science had demanded that he try alternate methods to find the answer to the puzzle he sought. They were in a neighborhood he wouldn't have come on his own, down by the wharves of East London, but all his logical deduction had led him to this conclusion.

"Two, please," Pippa said to young woman inside the little kiosk at the front of the theater, sliding several shilling coins across the counter.

The young woman pushed a button and several strips of rigid, white paper emerged from the machine underneath with a mechanical clunk. The woman pulled them clear and handed them to Pippa, leaning forward just a little so she could observe Royston, standing next to his daughter.

"Rock on, grandpa!" she called with a smile that did nothing to assuage the doubts plaguing Royston as to the rightness of this task.

Still, everything else had failed.

Royston Loughty, PhD, FRS, CBE, CStJ, had discovered enough new aspects of mathematics and physics in the last month to probably be considered for a Nobel Prize one of these days, and possibly the Fields Medal, but he had still failed in his intended task.

Gareth St. John Dankworth had disappeared from his cabin aboard *Shadow Base One*, the Arsenal, and nobody could explain how. Royston had even considered it to be perhaps a practical joke, but there was something there when he looked. Radiation signatures he could not explain with any science, in places that lent credence to the story and defied him in all other things.

Pippa, dearest only-daughter who reminded him too much of departed Elizabeth, had suggested baldly that obviously his understanding of physic was simply insufficient. Royston Loughty, possibly the greatest expert on Stellar Radiation in the entire Solar System, was out of his depth.

He had laughed then.

And yet.

Nights spent with a pad of paper, his favorite pipe, and a forgotten martini had gotten him nowhere. His favorite syncopated jazz music, from the bizarrely-experimental down to the coolest hep-cats, had left him cold. Rachmaninoff and Chopin, Tchaikovsky and Beethoven, even Gilbert and Sullivan. Nothing had provided him the inspiration he needed.

Royston escorted Pippa into the noisy auditorium on his left arm, as was proper. He felt desperately out of place here, wearing his traditional tweeds and a broad, silk tie that had been a gift from Pippa for some father's day long forgotten. Even his porkpie hat made him stand out in a room full of youngsters that probably considered Pippa an old maid at twenty-seven, with their slicked-back hair greased into pompadours made to look like little duck tails.

The mass of humanity around him probably had a median age of twenty, and he suspected an analysis of the mean would be even lower if he wishes to apply scientific procedures.

He did not.

Pippa was a bright spot of color, in her uniform as a Women's Auxiliary of Earth Force Sky Patrol. Crimson skirt just past her knees. Matching tunic as long as a blazer, double-breasted over the left with gold buttons and gold embroidery lacing. A yellow stripe edged the tunic and the collar, making her look like a professional woman, emphasizing the red hair and bright green eyes of her Scots heritage.

The children around them on all sides seemed to be in their own uniform. For the boys, blue dungarees, rolled up twice at the ankle. White T-shirts tucked in, frequently with a pack of cigarettes in the sleeve. Often a black jacket, sometimes leather and sometimes cotton denim.

The girls were identifiable by socio-economic class as Royston watched. Long poodle skirts gave way to simple skirts of a cut similar to Pippa's, growing progressively shorter until they barely covered more than a beach costume, as one tended down the scale of their father's income and profession. Finally, at what he considered the bottom, some daring souls were so androgynous as to ape the clothing of their male peers, even going so far as wearing pants in public.

Thankfully, Pippa's rebellious stage had never progressed farther than experiments in hair colors. Even his reputation might not have protected her, to be seen in dungarees, somewhere other than a farm.

They made their way to wooden, fold-down seats closer to the rear than the front of the auditorium. Three teenage-looking girls in too much makeup politely slid sideways a seat to make space for he and Pippa to sit together.

The youngster Royston found on his left looked up at him and then touched him silently on the arm with a smile, her palm placed flat in a welcoming gesture that left him perhaps both more and less terrified at the same time. Pippa's grin when he looked at her did nothing to assuage his embarrassment.

After a few moments, the lights came down and the restive crowd began to settle. Red velvet curtains across the stage withdrew slowly to the sides, revealing a band already in place, dressed in matching, slender black suits, with narrow ties and slicked back hair like so many of the men down front.

At the front, a young woman stood alone at a mic stand, eyeing the crowd like a predator stalking the high grass. She wore a turquoise, skin-tight dress, cut high on the sides to reveal too much thigh, like a nightclub's torch singer. Her long, brunette hair was wild and loose, billowing lightly in the breeze of a fan down front and centered up on her.

Black opera gloves covered her to elbows, and the dress itself was only to mid-thigh. At least she had sensible pumps on her feet, rather than the black, lace-up boots that she seemed to project with this image.

Royston tore his eyes aware from the mesmerizing female as the drummer began, a hard backbeat so at odds with the light brush of good jazz.

It was primal. Powerful. Unyielding.

After sixteen full measures, the crowd had fallen to utter silence, perhaps snakes charmed by the man with the pungi as they emerged from the darkness of the basket into the sun of this woman's music.

The bass player joined now, a harmonic beat walking back and forth on chords. His instrument was played upright in the classical style, but is was barely wider than the fretboard, with a plug emerging from the bottom to connect to the immense, black speaker stacks Royston saw threatening the crowd from both sides of the stage.

Two electric guitarists framed the woman, once closer to the front and one a step back, nearer in depth to the bass player. If he understood the mechanics and politics of the modern music, they represented a lead and rhythm guitar to offset the rhythm section of drums and bass. He did not see any horn players, so this would not be jazz as Royston understood the concept, but rock and roll.

He would survive the experience, come hell or high water.

A spotlight suddenly illuminated an upright piano off to one side, it's battered, wooden shell perhaps older than the young man playing it, as he slid a hand down from the top of the scale to draw all mesmerized eyes to the keys.

He began to play. No, that did not do the act justice.

The young man attacked the keyboard as though mortal combat had begun.

Hard, rhythmic, almost *bombastic*, if one could use that term to describe someone with the apparent technical chops to challenge Rachmaninoff instead throwing himself into rock and roll. Royston found his foot tapping with that back beat, head bobbing ever-so-slightly to the immense, lyrical complexities of the pianist.

One guitarist joined him. A full measure later, the other man gave meaning to the term *Lead Guitar* with a power and emotion that Royston had only known the best violinists and saxophonists to achieve. It was like a squall line had emerged from the stage and washed over the entire audience, a tide pushing them a little closer to shore, before the rip currents began to suck them out to sea.

And then the woman opened her mouth and sang.

Jazz was not generally known for its singers. The art form was in the instruments and the technical sophistication of the players. The few good scat singers had to work more to keep a hard beat with the musicians behind them, but rarely dominated, instead providing another piece of the rhythm section. Torch singers, on the other hand, were slow and emotionally-laden, immersing the hearer in sadness and longing.

This woman was power. Raw and unrestrained. Anger and love, sophistication and destruction.

It was like the ancient Hindu goddess Kali-ma stood before him on the stage, proclaiming the end of the world.

Somewhere in the middle of the performance, Royston noted that the singer had an easy working range of three octaves, and had touched four across the breadth of her songs.

At no point had a Master of Ceremonies emerged to work the crowd, and the woman never spoke. One song ended, everyone stopped to take a quick breath, drink some water while the crowd roared and clapped, and tune instruments.

And then the next song began, without even an explanation from the girl. Just the next notes in her ritual magic.

Royston felt one upbeat song end and the enchantress on stage transitioned into a love song that would have made the most embittered torch singer weep. He was suddenly nineteen again and meeting Elizabeth at that dance. In the middle of the first chorus, he realized that he had a young woman on each side leaning against him and weeping. Pippa and the unknown teenager had both unknowingly mirrored themselves, hooking an arm around his and pressing their heads against his shoulder while they listened.

As a sociological experiment, it was astonishing, but Royston did not move. Could not move. Both young women apparently needed something like this, and his mind was still too focused on the music, the syncopation, the skills on display. The raw emotions that the woman could invoke.

At the end of the song, Royston looked down at the young stranger on his left. She gazed up at him, blinked, and blushed so hard he thought she might pass out. He grinned a secret grin to her as she untangled herself and leaned away, lips pressed together to keep from speaking.

Pippa just grinned at his discomfort.

The woman on stage stood still in the quiet, and looked out over the audience. Her eyes seemed to find Royston in the stygian depths of the auditorium, boring into his soul with her medusa's gaze. Royston fell into darkness with the rest of the auditorium as the stage went dark, but for a single spotlight on the girl.

"One more," she intoned in a throating alto. "Best for last."

And it was. The previous hour had been a tour-de-force of emotional manipulation unlike anything Royston had ever witnessed, in any jazz bar or orchestra. The last song was Joshua at Jericho, bringing the very walls down with his music and the power of his faith.

Silence fell as the piano finally walked the last bits of tune away into the darkness. The spotlight went out and there was only darkness. Only emptiness.

Royston felt beads of sweat wick into his undershirt as his emotions tried to return to anything approximating normal. It would be hours before something so mundane was possible.

The lights came up suddenly and revealed the red, velvet curtains closed, sealing off the sorceress from her worshippers. The crowd of teenagers came alive and quickly made their way out of the auditorium, voices only slowly rising back to normal.

His was not the only soul in shock.

Even the teenager girl on his left stopped and gave him a chaste kiss on the cheek before turning and fleeing silently with her cohorts.

Within minutes, Royston found himself alone in the space, with only Pippa as company. She was withdrawn and quiet, but that was an understanding on her part that his brain was seeking some higher answers.

Finally, he rose, handing her to her feet.

Royston Loughty, PhD, FRS, CBE, CStJ, felt thirty, perhaps forty years younger. Energized in ways he could not remember.

He smiled at Philippa as he made his way to aisle.

Syncopated Jazz was a controlled thing. Technically sophisticated but somewhat emotionless. Symphonic music had more of the emotion, but it was filtered through a hundred musicians before it reached the audience.

This had been powerful. Primal. All the amazing skill of the best jazz musicians, but raw and uninhibited.

He nodded at Pippa and took her arm, emerging into the warm night at the tail end of the crowd.

"Did you find it?" she asked hesitantly. "Whatever it was that drew you here?"

"Perhaps," he replied quietly, drawing a breath of the magic deep into his lungs to take home with him to orbit.

Mathematics and physics were like jazz. Sophisticated and technical, without the powerful emotions that rock and roll brought to the table. They had not led him astray so much as merely fallen short of that place where his mind, his soul, needed to go.

He had needed rock and roll to show him the path.

Yes, perhaps he indeed had found the way.

HUNTERS

"HE DID WHAT?" Omerlon demanded angrily.

Rage drove the Elohynn to his feet, which was an impressive task, considering how far overweight Omerlon had grown, over the years. On bad days, his wings could barely lift him into the sky, and he didn't have the endurance to fly for long.

But no Elohynn ever walked.

That was why he had dedicated vehicles, customized to carry him around. That, and it was far easier to hide inside a closed vehicle than be out in the open where any goomba thug might take a shot at him. Or narc him to the cops.

This vehicle had been converted from a panel van, giving him three meter ceilings and a thick, brown shag rug. He used it to pace right now. They still had time before arrival at the next destination.

The Warreth stayed seated across the way cringed, but didn't clam up.

"Reporters got a tip, boss," Danzeekar replied. "Damabiath had been tied to a chair and his left wing had been stripped to the flesh. Not a single feather left. And he was dead."

Omerlon hissed in rage. There was no greater insult anyone could give to an Elohynn. None. Anywhere. Bodies would pile up at the morgue over something like this. His Warreth captain agreed, from the set of his headcrest and the way his feathers all puffed out a little.

"And Maximus did it?" Omerlon snarled. "We have confirmation?"

"I got someone close to his inner circle, feeding us tidbits now and again," Danzeekar replied. "Never much, but never wrong in the past. They know which way the wind is blowing, but can't get out right now. Maximus is a wild card and nobody's sure what he'll do next."

"If he wants a war, I'll give him one," Omerlon growled.

All his life, he had been an outsider kid. Too heavy compared to those sleek bastards at the aerie who made fun of him. Too short. Too ugly.

Always too something.

He didn't know if he had been born broken and didn't find out until later, or if the anger had just built up over enough years and twisted something inside him. Most people couldn't kill someone without a lot of anguish up front, as well as afterwards.

Omerlon had gotten over that crap pretty quick. It had gotten him in with a series of ever-more-dangerous criminal gangs, until he ended up in charge of the biggest on *Orgoth Vortai*. An Elohynn ruling an underworld largely composed of Grace, but still the dregs of any society.

Omerlon stopped pacing and turned to face Danzeekar. They would be close to their destination and landing soon. He needed time to get himself together and look the part of the lord of the underworld, especially if he had to go to war with Maximus.

"Do we know where the bastard's hiding?" Omerlon asked quietly, his voice honed down to a razor's rusty edge.

"Negative on that, boss," Danzeekar said. "I get my notes third-hand through delivery boys right now. Hasn't been worth trying to push back up the chain yet, because we're likely to blow our mole and it hasn't been that important yet."

"And it still isn't," Omerlon decided.

He flexed his head back and snapped a shudder through his wings to loosen them up. Had there been space in here, he would have run them out to points. He would probably need that level of intimidation shortly, especially with some of the people around here having second thoughts.

"Find me those two physicists that disappeared," Omerlon ordered. "We'll use them as bait to bring Maximus to us, and then crush that weasel."

"You got it, boss," Danzeekar nodded.

Outside, Omerlon felt the truck shift as it started its descent. The Mayor of Londra, the biggest city, needed to be reminded how little wiggle room he had if he wanted to stay out of jail, and keep his entire, corrupt family free with him.

Omerlon looked forward to venting some of his spleen on the bastard. Maximus wasn't going to get away with killing his people.

34

FUGITIVE

"HEARD ANY NEWS?" Morty asked as he emerged from his bedroom.

Xiomber looked up from his morning paper, tea mug in one hand and a sour scowl on his face as he sat in the dining space and enjoyed his quiet.

"News news, or real stuff?" Xiomber asked.

Morty walked over to join his egg-brother at the table. The place was cheap, but their needs weren't all that great right now. And a month on the run had given Morty a far-greater appreciation of the simple things in life, like hot food that didn't come out of a convenience store refrigerator. And a roof over his head when it was raining.

The table even a had a pretty good view of the city from about seventy stories up. *Churquark* was the name of both the city and the planet. It was mainly a Grace world, so there was art everywhere, but the window next to the kitchen table looked out over a two hundred meter tall bronze statue of a Chaa, one of the Elders, poised apparently at that moment of awakening that had transformed them from amazingly-advanced scientists into gods.

And that wasn't even the weirdest thing Morty could see from here, as he pulled up a seat and poured himself some tea.

"Whatever news you got, Xiomber," Morty replied to his partner. "You always wake up at dawn and scour the boards and papers for things. I need my beauty sleep."

"Ain't that the truth?" Xiomber nodded.

Morty just grinned and let his egg-brother's sarcasm roll off his scales. He was feeling especially feisty this morning.

"So talk to me," Morty prompted.

"We been here three days, Morty," Xiomber sighed.

"And we've been on the run for five weeks," Morty countered. "Maximus ain't taken over the galaxy in that time, and nobody's heard anything about Gareth or Talyarkinash, so either they got away, or the Constables really did catch them and have been hiding them someplace."

"We better hope that the Constables didn't catch them then," Xiomber paused and sipped his tea noisily, like an alligator running low in the water, eyes and snout above the steam. "Prices for gear had gone through the roof on the black market."

"Everything?" Morty felt a metaphorical scorpion perch on his shoulder and eye the side of his head hungrily. Never a good way to wake up.

"Everything we would need to build a new lab,"

Xiomber explained. "Generators, control surfaces, secondary coils, even the sensors like we used to locate Sarzynski and Dankworth in the first place."

"They know the truth, then," Morty was sure.

"That's my guess, too," his partner nodded. "Somebody rolled, or maybe they finally raided the palace back on *Zathus*. Rumor on the street was that Maximus shut the place down when you and I bailed, and nobody cleaned it up afterwards. Wouldn't take much to put two and two together, ya know?"

"No way to build a new lab?" Morty asked, just in case.

"Not an underground one," Xiomber said. "And I'm guessing all the legitimate physicists in the family are probably cursing our names right now for the amount of paperwork they suddenly have to go through to replace or upgrade anything."

Morty shrugged. Small price to pay, if they wanted to ensure that the *Accord of Souls* was still here in a year.

Ya burn the house down, you don't get to complain about sleeping in the backyard when it rains. Summoning a human like Maximus had to be the dumbest idea he'd ever let himself be talked into. Summoning Gareth to stop him had perhaps balanced the scales a little. Hopefully enough.

If the Chaa really were gods, he was going to have to do a lot of hand-waving, when he got to his final reward. Angry deities weren't going to be happy at what he had done to the galactic commons they had carefully built and arranged before leaving. And they sure weren't going to like humans running around outside their house.

"Any good news from all that?" Morty continued after a moment of thought.

"We're connected into the underground here," Xiomber said in a careful voice.

"But?"

"But both the Constables and Maximus are hunting our asses, Morty," his egg-brother said. "And offering threats and rewards that are going to get somebody to roll on us, eventually."

"You're the street etiquette expert," Morty replied. "Is there anybody who could protect us? I'm willing to work for my keep, as long as they don't go down Cinnra's path and decide they need more humans. Even cops. At some point, someone will talk."

"Or a human will walk into a teashop and get tasted by a Grace?" Xiomber sneered.

"Hey, you left him alone, too," Morty said. "If she knows what he tastes like, my greatest hope is that the cops scared the wits out of the girl. You saw what that Vanir chick was like when she took off after Gareth."

"Yeah," Xiomber shuddered, eyes flickering with memory. "Ain't going there again."

"So find us someplace to set up shop," Morty said. "Even half-legit works for me. I haven't completely forgotten how to write code for responsible companies. I really don't want to have to go back to *Yuudix* and hide among a billion grains of sand. Don't think that would stop the Constabulary."

Xiomber nodded in agreement. He started to say something when his pocketcomm beeped.

The two Yuudixtl looked at each other for a moment, and then Xiomber shrugged and answered it.

"They're your kopeks," he said into the phone and then listened.

"Yeah?" Xiomber said a moment later. "Okay. Thanks. I owe you one for that. Later."

He hung up and stared at Morty

"We got a problem."

OFFICER OF THE COURT

GARETH WALKED into the briefing room expecting to find a mob waiting. Instead, he found an empty conference room with Talyarkinash Liamssen quietly waiting, sipping from what smelled like a glass of juice from here. Gareth blushed slightly as he realized that no human, nor Vanir, should be able to smell that well. Even a Nari like her might be hard pressed to match it.

And yet.

She rose as he entered and stepped away from the big, rectangular table to hug him. Nothing more, just physical contact that she seemed to find reassuring. If Gareth had given up everything in order to stop Maximus, Talyarkinash had come close in terms of cost.

She had lost her entire existence, being arrested at the same time Gareth was and quickly disappeared into police custody. However, she had been a willing witness once everything was explained to her, turning over names and addresses to the two Constables. It was the least she could do to help undo all the evil she had done, unwittingly or not.

She had burned all bridges, but still had a future in front of her. She was still Nari. Still five-foot-eight, approaching six feet at the tips of her ears. Her Imperial Blue fur was still sleek and shiny with gorgeous stripes, complimenting her eyes. Gareth had even gotten used to a woman with bigger and more luxurious muttonchop sideburns than any man he had ever known could grow.

He would have guessed that the Chaa, the Elder race responsible for the *Accord of Souls*, had taken a Canadian Lynx and transformed it into a woman-like creature. The eyes slitted vertically. The snout was ever-so-slightly prominent. She smiled with teeth that had more points than his did when she smiled at him.

But she had become a friend. And he, hers. She would have gone to prison forever, according to the Constables, but for her willingness to work with them to understand everything she had done to Gareth. And what some greater fool might do, next time.

Someone like Marc Sarzynski.

Gareth took his seat and considered coffee. Or whatever the thing in the silver urn on the side table should actually be called. It was close enough for his taste buds, raised on the instant stuff kept in a big can in the freezer, rather than freshly-roasted beans ground on demand.

Sounded like too much work. Like shaving had turned into as his beard came in. Or getting his hair cut.

Gareth wondered if he was going through teenage rebellion, or a very early mid-life crisis. Being turned into a giant alien creature would probably have that effect on a guy.

The side door opened before Gareth could decide. Eveth Baker and Jackeith Grodray entered, and nobody else. Just the four of them in the room.

He looked around the room at the other three people with an inside giggle. He and the two Constables were all wearing the exact same uniform, the steel blue bodysuit with triangular scales. Grodray had added the outer tunic that made him look more formal, while he and Baker had not.

Talyarkinash was wearing purple. Skin-tight, cheongsam top without any sleeves. Baggy, Samurai pants in a broad straight-leg cut, with a high waist that flared out at the top, almost like a pirate girdle. Everything she wore was embroidered with silver, in some arcane design that almost looked like something he had seen once in a Shia Mosque in Samarkand.

"What's so funny?" Baker asked as she took the seat directly across from Gareth.

She wasn't angry. Or it wasn't at him, anyway. At last not that he could tell.

Grodray had ended up across from the Nari woman, but his face was more closed.

"Wondering if there was any symbolism in fashion," Gareth replied.

It didn't make any sense, but she had asked.

Baker looked like she wanted to say something, then looked like she was trying not to roll her eyes at him. Finally, she huffed once and settled.

"Will it be just us today?" Talyarkinash asked in a serious voice, dividing her attention between the two.

Eveth Baker was probably the more dangerous, from a purely physical standpoint, although Gareth had been her match back when he's still been human. Grodray was still a more interesting foe from a strategic standpoint. He only looked like a Senior Constable, a role he played to mislead watchers. The man was really a Prime Investigator, a free agent allowed by his superiors to go wherever the crime might lead him.

As far as Gareth knew, Baker wasn't one. Not yet, but she had something like a candidate status, so she probably would be in another year or so, if all went well.

Gareth really didn't know where he fit into the whole mess. Talyarkinash was at least a scientist, and had been working closely with some of the staff here, but only a few people and most of them were not *read fully into* the project that was Gareth St. John Dankworth, renegade human, genetically-engineered monster.

Baker paused and looked deliberately at Grodray.

The older man suddenly looked angry enough to chew nails, where he had just been serious before.

"The fewer people that are aware of this operation, the better," Grodray said ominously.

Gareth heard the echoes of vast, bureaucratic arguments in the background of those words. Complaints taken all the way to the highest authority, rather than being worked out down in the trenches.

When you have a human on the loose, things could get ugly. Two of them doubled the problems.

"How can we help?" Gareth asked the man simply.

That was why they were here. Nothing else would require the two of them to physically travel this far, when they could send a message or a courier.

"I understand from Dr. Liamssen that you have gained better control of your…powers," Grodray began.

Gareth nodded silently.

"I need to see you in action, Gareth," the Senior Constable said. "That will tell me what I need to know about how to use you, going forward."

"Here?" he asked.

"No," Grodray said. "Too many witnesses. We need to go up-country to the gunnery range. I've had it locked down for the next two days, so there will be nobody but us."

Gareth whistled unconsciously at the astounding display of authority in those words. He caught the slightest flinch in Baker as well. Talyarkinash had never been in part of a major bureaucracy, so didn't understand that it was almost never possible to simply snap your fingers and just have something *happen*.

"I can go whenever," he said, turning to the Nari woman next to him. "Talyarkinash?"

"I suspected that was why you were here," she allowed. "I have some equipment in my lab that we will need, specially prepared for Gareth when he's in the field."

"What kind of equipment?" Baker spoke up now.

"When he transforms, his clothing and anything he is carrying somehow become absorbed into the new form, and then returned to normal later," Talyarkinash replied. "After a month, I still don't understand it, but humans have vast, latent psionic powers that might eventually put them on a par with the Chaa."

"And?" Baker almost growled.

"So the first round of bio-sensors I put on him went perfectly blank for the entire time he was transformed. Constable Baker," the Nari woman returned the challenge. "I have a new design that I want to try. Hopefully it will work. Science is about attempting and failing until you succeed. I do not know if I am there, yet, but I am getting closer."

"Oh." Baker backed off, which Gareth found rather interesting.

She was a big woman. Slender and athletic, but muscular and a whole head taller than the scientist. However, she was apparently willing to learn, and maybe even admit when she was wrong, or maybe pushing a little too hard.

"Gareth?" Baker asked.

Which was kind of astounding, but he hoped he hid it well. Usually, she only called him Dankworth to his face.

"Whatever you need, Constable," Gareth replied evenly. "Maximus is still out there."

SCIENTIST

IF THE GODS would have allowed it, Talyarkinash would have rebuilt herself to be seven feet tall, just so she could lurk above Eveth Baker for once, to give the woman a dose of her own medicine. Among her own kind, Talyarkinash was usually an inch taller than any Nari woman she met.

Being around Vanir all the time was wearing on the soul.

She kept her grumbles to herself though, as she climbed into the Constabulary Transport and buckled herself in, followed by the three giants from some fairy tale. Her small equipment bag, almost a purse, went between her feet.

Gareth was the most perfect gentleman. Had been from the first moment they had met. Had remained so even after she had discovered he was human. He gave lie to all those horrible threats and fairy tales her mother had told her as a kitten, even going so far as to confirm her seatbelt was done before attaching his own harness when he got in just now.

Baker, on the other hand, had been a major burr in her tailfur from the beginning.

Talyarkinash was willing to allow that she had been with the bad guys at the time. And guilty of some of the worst crimes on the books. Technically. Conspiracy and Being an Accessory to Treason were not particularly good things to list on her C.V., so she was planning on leaving those off, if she ever managed to make to a class reunion.

At least one outside prison. She had a pretty good idea how many of her old associates would probably be able to make one of those in another few years.

Eveth Baker was a bully. Emotionally. Psychologically. Even physically. It made her a good cop, Talyarkinash supposed. It also made her a pain in the ass, most of the time.

At least Baker appeared to be completely immune to the charms of one Gareth St. John Dankworth. That helped.

Gareth still had the card from some other Nari woman in his wallet. Seriously, the woman had given a complete stranger from another species a scent card.

What the hell?

Not that Talyarkinash hadn't considered doing the same, from time to time. Being human, Gareth had just possessed a magnetism that would have made her rich, had she been able to identify it, bottle it, and market it. After becoming Vanir, it was all she could do some days to not run her fingertips through his mane.

The craft lifting off concealed the way her fingers curled in her lap.

Post-zenith sun in a clear sky out the windows. Cool up here from the elevation, but she could have found a place out of the breeze, if she wanted to just bask on a warm rock. Instead, she had added a jacket that hung to her knees and a wool-lined cap with the perfect ear holes, for when they got even further up the enormous valley and the temperatures began to nip, even in direct sunlight.

This much wilderness was unnatural to a city kitten like her, but it was the hand she had been dealt. Rumors had been circulating that Maximus was currently in a war with his own people, deep in the underworld, to retain control. Or regain it. She was much safer with Baker and Grodray protecting her.

And Gareth.

If she was in the city, any city, someone would have found her, eventually. Maximus had done some amazingly savage things, even for a human, according to Gareth. She would have been on Sarzynski's list. Especially from where the two of them had started, her and Maximus.

Much better here.

The flight took all of about fifteen long, silent minutes. Gareth was lost in his sightseeing. Baker was scowling at something, but she always did. Grodray had grown introspective.

Gareth had explained to her the armies of earlier centuries on Earth. The tremendous wars fought over things she still couldn't quite parse. But more importantly, the science of destruction that his species had worshipped for so many millennia and the amazing advances they had driven in human culture, over just a few millennia.

Bronze Age to Space in three thousand years? Without outside intervention? Amazing.

And frightening. Where would they be in another thousand years?

The Gunnery Range they were about to take over was designed to give Heavy Rescue teams from the Constabulary a place to practice, working with weapons that could kill, rather than just stun, when you needed to blow things up, or destroy vehicles.

When you were reduced to the sorts of savagery that humans apparently just took for granted.

Talyarkinash shuddered, in spite of herself as they landed.

She had been here twice before, working with Gareth as he flew and practiced things like the breath weapon he had insisted almost all human cultures expected that dragons were born with.

Was there a more violent species, anywhere in the galaxy?

Today, the place was abandoned. Completely empty.

Even the vehicle bringing them had been auto-piloted, so the four of them might be the only people within twenty kilometers in any direction.

The old Talyarkinash would have had serious qualms about that sort of situation. Too easy to be brought up here and vanish without any trace that a crime had been committed. But Baker and Grodray weren't that sort of cops. And there was Gareth.

This might be one of the few situations in her life that Talyarkinash was confident she could take at face value.

She turned in place to view the magnificent arena formed by a bowl of mountains all the way around her as she emerged. The tarmac where they had parked was probably over one thousand hectares by itself, with a line of six enormous hangars on the right and a set of office buildings and warehouses on the left. Space for five, or maybe eight thousand people in a pinch, although last time she had been here, the population had been barely two dozen, sworn to secrecy but still gawking in the afternoon sun at a bronze dragon flying overhead. At least they had all had an occasional friendly smile for her.

The air was crisp, but not enough to penetrate her coat. If a breeze picked up, the hat would go on, but she was fine for now. It even smelled faintly of pine sap, a sticky, green pungency at the lower end of her range. Gareth almost certainly could detect it, but she doubted the cops would be able to.

That brought the faintest smile to her face as she fell in behind Grodray, with the other two behind her.

He led the column to a tower, a five story square cylinder where flight control would be able to see aircraft coming and going, and keep them organized in the sort of emergency where auto-pilots might not be smart enough to all maneuver in synch.

The stairs warmed her, as did being inside, to the point she pulled her coat open and considered taking it off.

Talyarkinash found the echoes in the stairwell

amusing. Grodray walked with a lighter step than most Vanir, while Baker seemed to be trying to punish each tread as she stepped on it. Gareth made almost no sound, just a whisper more than she did.

The step into the brightness of the top chamber, after the dimness of the stairwell, caused her eyes to slam nearly shut for a moment, before they flickered sideways again.

Empty.

Four sides where up to eight controllers could work, although one was normal. She followed Grodray to the side where they had the best view of the long runway. He turned and gave them his best grouchy stare.

"Wanted to confirm we were completely alone," he said simply. "Dr. Liamssen, you said you had mechanisms that would not necessarily be part of Gareth's translation?"

"I do," she said, reaching into the bag she had brought with her and pulling out a small, clamshelled container that she handed to Gareth. "Attach this to your ear like an earring, and flip the tip into your ear canal."

He took it and opened the box warily. Simple enough, for now. A clip for the cartilage, hinged. He pulled it out and put it on. She saw a little red light appear.

Talyarkinash pulled out the communicator and pressed the button that would send a beep. He nodded in response, so she handed it to Grodray.

"Gareth's side is voice activated," she said. "Press the button on the side when you want to talk."

"Gareth, I've seen the videos of you in action," Grodray said. "I've read Dr. Liamssen's reports, plus a few others from around you. Those were relaxed, controlled circumstances. I want to see you in something like combat circumstances. Questions?"

"Anything in particular?" Gareth asked, himself falling into the seriousness of the other cops.

"Speed, maneuverability, fire," Grodray said. "We're reaching a point where talk now is about putting you in the field to hunt Sarzynski."

"Stalking horse?" Gareth asked.

"Do you know a better way to hunt lions?"

Talyarkinash shuddered. Maximus was at least that dangerous. Hopefully Gareth was as well.

DRACO-FORM

GARETH EMERGED from the bottom of the tower and sniffed the air around him. Nobody. It was odd, being able to smell like a hunting dog when he concentrated.

The base had been occupied until recently, but everyone had left at least a day ago. All this, just for him.

"Checking in," he said, assuming that the earpiece would pick it up.

"Go ahead, Gareth," Grodray said.

Deep breath. Reach down and grasp hold of the power that Talyarkinash had placed inside his soul when she given him the ability to transform. It no longer hurt as much to turn. Instead, it was a friendly heat that wrapped around him like hands, rather than scorching them. Even the pain of transformation was manageable.

Gareth paused, and took a second breath. The fire seemed to engulf him physically, although he had seen videos where he transformed, and everything was internal.

Just his imagination that he was burning.

And his perception changed as well. Eyes moved outward as his skull reshaped, granting him peripheral vision almost good enough to see all directions at once. Chitin formed from his blood and bone created a ridge of dragon plates that ran back his skull and all the way down to the new tail that was extending outward.

Fortunately, the uniform really did subsume itself into his flesh. The first attempt Talyarkinash had given him had shredded under the stress, coming apart and leaving him naked when he shifted back.

Dragons could blush, but right now nobody could see it under the bronze scales covering his face. He smiled, as much as he could with the new form of his jaw, too much like the Yuudixtl who had been his inspiration.

Crocodile smile.

"Can you still read me, Constable Grodray?" Gareth asked, his voice rumbling a rich bass in his own ears.

"Affirmative, Dankworth," the man replied. "Go ahead."

Gareth took several running steps and threw himself at the sky. He could fly from a standstill, pumping heavily to gain altitude, but this was much more efficient, using the tiny amount of breeze to gain a little lift.

Quickly, he was twenty meters in the air, racing along at sixty kilometers per hour as he rose higher.

Grodray had given him no directions, other than to show off, so Gareth decided to stretch his abilities today.

Up and up, slowly orbiting the tower as a central beacon for his column, until he was nearly a thousand meters in the air. He rolled over and aimed himself to glide a little, back along the runway back to where their transport was parked.

There were a few birds up this high, but most had fled at the sight of the monstrous, strange beast breaking up the afternoon sky. A few predators continued to circle at what they thought might be a safe distance, but even they kept their orbits far wider than his, reacting like scalded cats when he turned one way or the other.

Finally, he turned, finding the line of the runway and pulling his wings in until just the tips stuck out, like tiny ailerons providing him control as he nosed over into freefall. Below, the equivalents of eagles and hawks scattered to the four winds with surprised cries.

Gareth rumbled a laugh, forgetting for a moment that the microphone was live.

"Everything okay?" Grodray asked, but it sounded more like a formality than anything.

"Speed drop," Gareth replied. "Locals are a little nervous."

"Roger that."

His draco-form was streamlined. The final size he had reached when he had stopped growing as a Vanir was twenty-seven meters from sleek snout to spiky tail. Pulled in tight, he quickly reached a terminal velocity far greater than a human skydiver ever could.

And he had learned early on how much torque his wings could take before they buckled under the stress, so he slowly stretched his wings out, forcing his flight flatter and flatter as he went, transforming into the horizontal from the vertical that he had started.

He didn't have an airspeed indicator gauge to track his speed, but his inner eyelid had dropped down, making everything just the slightest bit fuzzy while still letting him track large targets. Still, Talyarkinash had built him a communicator.

What else might it do?

"Can you track my airspeed?" Gareth asked as he flattened out and pumped his wings to keep him level and running, about twenty meters above the concrete apron below.

He would pass below his audience, if he was careful.

"Two hundred and eighty kph, Gareth," Talyarkinash replied after a few seconds. "Peak during your dive was three hundred and fifteen."

Wow. Faster than anything on the ground, and fast enough to catch most flying vehicles under computer control.

For fun, Gareth pulled back a little and shifted into an Immelmann maneuver, holding his wings still as he went straight up and stalled. An aircraft losing forward momentum like this would have to flip over and undo a stall, falling initially onto its tail.

Here, Gareth started his stall like normal, and then

folded himself in two, pulling his wings in, reversing course like a diver coming off the high board. After a moment, he extended his wings again and flapping hard enough to hover in place fifty meters in the air.

For fun, he slowly pivoted on his tail at the same time, until he was facing the threesome in the tower from around seventy-five meters away, like the galaxy's biggest hummingbird.

Not the meanest. Hummingbirds back home had attitudes like tiny T-Rexes, all bluster and fury, while still small enough to fit in your hand. He could gulp one down in a single bite if they decided to get feisty with him today.

Let's see, speed, maneuverability, and hover displayed.

Gareth winged over and landed, more or less below the control tower window. Glancing up, he could see three faces leaned out and looking down, so he reared back and triggered the two glands in his upper chest, pressing out paired streams of liquid that ran up into his mouth.

One turned into a spray, and then the second mixed with it and ignited, reacting to the oxygen in the air and the misty spray to turn into a column of fire nearly thirty meters long for a second. There was nothing to burn, but he knew he would leave a scorch mark on the concrete that newcomers couldn't explain.

Folks who had been there to watch him before would know. He was sure rumors were already floating about the *Accord of Souls*.

Fire-breathing-dragon. Gareth was pretty sure that

both Grace and Nari would react with the same awe and trepidation as humans did.

"Did you need a strength demonstration?" Gareth rumbled. "I could lift one end of the transport, but I don't think I could get the whole thing off of the ground."

"That's okay, Gareth," Grodray was back on line. "Go ahead and return to normal for now. I want to talk about next steps."

Gareth had landed on all fours for stability. He reared up now and let go of the terrible fire in his soul, feeling the energy collapse back down inside somewhere.

Talyarkinash had said that the ability was psionic, whatever that meant. Except that he didn't have any biology or physics that could explain what he did. Neither did she.

Magic was as good a description an anything, he supposed. He wondered if Dr. Loughty would be able to do any better, but he doubted it, as far beyond Terran culture and technology as he found himself these days.

Still, he was happy when he looked down and his skin was covered in a blue scaled jumpsuit. He had believed the Nari scientist and her equipment, but there was always that least bit of doubt in the back of his mind.

Grodray emerged first, with Baker close on his heels. Talyarkinash was several seconds behind, but she probably went down every step, when the taller twosome didn't have to. Not necessarily fair, but not a lot he could do about it.

"I had to see it with my own eyes," Grodray said by way of apology. He held out a hand for Gareth to shake.

"Understood, sir," Gareth replied. "I still don't always believe it myself. What's next?"

Something in the man's face was off, the way Grodray's eyes found Talyarkinash and he lost all emotion.

"Field work," he said.

Gareth was confused. Doubly so when Talyarkinash smiled.

PRIME INVESTIGATORS

EVETH WAITED until they had returned Dankworth and Liamssen to the base, and then cleared that on their way back to town.

"Out with it," Grodray said from the bench across from her. "You've been stewing for an hour, and too polite to say anything in front of those two. What's eating you?"

"Is he ready?" she asked simply, compacting any number of arguments into those few words. Grodray was her boss, and a Prime Investigator, however secret that designation was. He made his own job, as he saw fit.

And the highest echelons of the *Accord of Souls* would back him. She could have opinions, but she was only a candidate to become a Prime Investigator herself, so she needed to be a team player right now, working within Grodray's framework.

Grodray surprised her by smiling.

"Not really sure it matters, Eve," he said. "I'm up to no good here."

"How so?" she asked, a little lost.

Normally, Jackeith Grodray was deduction itself. Cold, calculating, logical. That was one of the reasons she had been given about why she'd initially been paired with the man, as her own approach was much more inductive. She could make fantastic, intuitive leaps, so he balanced her, so the story went.

Since the mask had come off, revealing that a well-respected Senior Constable, a simple Level Four, who was actually a Level Seven, she had seen a side of the man she had never really imagined.

"Playing a couple of hunches," Grodray said.

"You?"

He laughed and leaned back into the chair with a twinkle in his eyes.

"One, Maximus has a deep and abiding hatred of Gareth," Grodray said. "You've read the debriefing reports and the bio that Gareth helped assemble on the man."

"Stalking horse," Eveth replied, nodding with understanding. "Put him out in the open and see if you can draw Sarzynski out of the shadows to take a shot at him."

"Correct," Jackeith nodded. "But there's a second element at play, and I want to see how that works."

"What's that?" Eveth pressed. What else could there be?

"I've watched a number of female officers and researchers around Gareth," Grodray said. "Plus the original reports, and that young woman in the tea shop when he was first pulled through to *Orgoth Vortai*."

"What about him?" she asked bluntly.

"And that's the best part," Grodray said with a dry chuckle. "You appear to be immune, but every other female Gareth Dankworth comes into contact with has a serious, visceral reaction to the man. And they did even when he was human, but becoming Vanir hasn't changed it."

"The fact that every woman wants to jump his bones?" Eveth asked.

"Except you," her partner grinned.

"He's human, Jack," she snapped, finding a seam of coal underneath her words to ignite. "That's disgusting."

"They don't know that," he countered. "And if it works, I want to turn him loose in a few places, to see if that charm and magnetism can get us into a few areas where pure police work has failed."

"And if it does?" she sneered.

"Then he breaks our case even further open, Eve," the man turned serious. "I'll get all the glory on this one, but you're doing the hard work, and you'll get credit in the right places."

She liked that thought. On the one hand, that would be her ticket into the big leagues.

And maybe, if she was lucky, the two humans would manage to wipe each other out and save everyone else a lot of trouble.

OMELETS

IT WAS GETTING OLD.

Morty knew they were in the top ten most wanted people in the entire *Accord of Souls*, but it would be nice to be able to stay in the same apartment for more than a week before somebody tipped either the cops or his old friends from *Zathus*, as to where he and Xiomber were staying.

Today, supposedly, it had been the bad guys who got the call.

Fortunately, Xiomber had friends. Or was owed enough favors. Or maybe owed enough other people that they wanted to be able to collect on those debts in the future and couldn't if he was dead.

Whatever. The phone had rung. A message had been conveyed. And they ran like hell for the door.

Somewhere, there was still a pot of tea cooling on a kitchen table with a fantastic view of that giant bronze statue: *"Walking into Discovery."* It was a stupid name for a piece of art, but the Grace were weirdoes to begin with, so he wasn't going to argue.

And Xiomber had found them a nice dive on the edge of downtown to get breakfast. Not too close to the old place, where someone might see them accidentally, but only three stops away on the first bus that had driven by.

Fortunately, after a month on the run, Morty's entire life pretty much fit into a single bag. He had a few bolt holes scattered around the *Accord*, and he and Xiomber had set up a few joint efforts beyond that, but these days it really was possible to grab his comm off the counter, and his bag by the door, and walk out of an apartment forever.

"So who called?" Morty asked as the waiter delivered menus and a fresh pot of tea.

They were seated clear down at the back of the narrow joint, tucked into a tiny table that was invisible from the front door and most of the windows, back around where the counter wrapped and led to the restrooms. The joint had been decorated in white: walls, counter, floor, aprons; but it still had a dinginess that no amount of soap would ever get out. Too many cigarettes and plates of greasy bacon and eggs had passed through here over the years.

And the crowd was just starting to wind themselves up, but Morty could see three tables left for whoever managed to get here next. After that, he was pretty sure the line would be out the door, just from the smells coming from the kitchen.

Seriously, there were what looked like a couple of

farmers at the counter, enjoying a break between milking cows and whatever else folks like that did in the morning. Except they had to have come all the way into town to eat here, because the nearest farms were like thirty kilometers away. Above them, a television was showing two pretty talking heads doing morning news and fluff, but the sound was off.

Morty studied the menu while Xiomber ruminated on the question he had posed.

"Nobody you know," Xiomber finally said. "Old girlfriend I did striped scales for, back when she got married."

"Ah, her," Morty said. "She must still like you?"

"Enough," Xiomber allowed with a vague shrug. "She got a whisper and put two and two together."

"Do we need to get off this rock?" Morty asked, pouring some tea and letting it warm his mug.

"I don't think we're totally screwed yet," his egg-brother nodded, pouring his own tea. "The old gang didn't have many fingers here, so finding us requires that they use the locals. People will talk."

"Yeah, but how soon until you run out of friends, or they get lucky?" Morty asked.

Xiomber shrugged.

"I had hoped that we could drop down the rabbit hole here, Morty," he said. "Find someone to take us on faith and let us work for them for a while, at least until the heat died down, ya know?"

"The old man's getting more desperate, not less," Morty noted. "You saw what he did to Damabiath. I don't want to know what a scaleless Yuudixtl looks like, m'kay?"

A sudden sound caught them both short, a low moan of surprise and shock rippling through the crowd. Morty and Xiomber both turned, but Morty had to half-stand out of his seat to see over the counter and know what was going on.

All heads had turned to the television screen over the counter, by the front door.

"Turn up the sound," somebody yelled.

A Warreth waitress fumbled with a remote control for a few seconds before she found the right buttons.

"…repeating our top story, an explosion occurred just a few minutes ago in a downtown apartment tower, blowing out windows across the street, but apparently confined to just one apartment. Fire and police are responding, and we've got the first images from our **Morning Three** *Eye In The Sky* drone," the female, a Grace, was saying.

The image was zoomed in on a blackened window, smoke oozing out, before the camera pulled back to show the rest of the tower and part of the street. The operator slowly rotated the hovering camera in place to show windows shattered, but it looked like a pretty clean explosion.

It helped that tower blocks like this were generally self-contained reinforced-concrete shells. All the boom would tend to go outward, and usually a fire would be contained to just one flat. Defensive architecture was a hallmark of the *Accord*. Keep everybody safe.

Morty blew the air out of his lungs and sat down hard, muttering profanities under his breath.

"Yeah," Xiomber said. "I saw the same thing. Now I'm really glad we left when we did."

Morty wasn't sure exactly how somebody had killed their apartment. Explosive shaped charge on the front door? Missile in through the kitchen window?

Maybe they had kicked in the door, found that Morty and his egg-brother gone, then lost their temper? Morty would have been tempted to stake the place out, on the off-chance that the two fugitives would return, but apparently Maximus and his people already knew they had flown the coop.

That looked like a message. And an unpleasant one.

Morty sighed and picked up the menu.

"We owe your old girlfriend big time," he muttered.

"That's exactly what she said," Xiomber smiled back grimly. "She said it would probably make the morning news, whatever it was, and we should walk out immediately. Thoughts?"

"Omelet with everything," Morty replied absently. "Gimme lots of carbs and protein this morning because I got a feeling it's only going to get worse from here."

"I meant about us," Xiomber groused.

"That's what I'm talking about," Morty snapped. "I'm beginning to wonder if we're out of rope, Xiomber. Like we have to finally do something amazingly stupid if we want to survive all this. Lots of broken eggs in our future."

Xiomber's eyes slitted down tight, and his lids dropped halfway.

"How stupid?" he asked.

The waiter interrupted at that moment. Morty went all in, obviously afraid that this might be his last nice meal for a while, and he could always stuff the other half into a to-go box and carry it with him for lunch.

Xiomber started easy, but saw something in Morty's eyes that appeared to unsettle him. He ordered the ribeye with eggs and hash, instead of a fruit and greens salad. The waiter smiled and departed.

"How stupid?" Xiomber repeated, but his heart wasn't filled with anger. Morty could see that.

"Let's find Gareth," he said quietly.

"You know who has him," Xiomber snapped, keeping his own voice as low as possible.

"Yeah," Morty acknowledged. "But I'd rather spend the next forty years complaining that I've read the entire prison library than be dead by lunchtime, okay? We can always get ourselves rehabilitated later."

"You think they'll let us out of prison in this lifetime, egg-brother?" Xiomber sneered.

"The crazy lizard who started all this has had a significant change of heart, brother," Morty said. "I screwed up, big time, and nearly brought the entire *Accord of Souls* down. I own that, yes, but I've spent the last two months trying to save civilization from all those crazy bastards. Do you want an immortal super-human ruling the *Accord* for the rest of time? No. Hell,

I'd be happy if anyone ever figured out how to summon back the Chaa and let them fix everything."

"You'd be in hell, Morty," his brother said. "And I'd be with you."

"And the galaxy would survive, Xiomber," he snapped. "Maximus would be dealt with. Gareth's people would either be stuffed back into their hole or modified enough to be added to the *Accord*. People like you and I could go back to whatever petty crime and juvenile shenanigans the Elders left us as crumbs if they didn't just wipe us from existence. But the galaxy would be *safe*."

"Gareth?" Xiomber asked morosely after a moment. "You realize all the cops on this planet are pretty bent, right?"

"Yeah," Morty said. "I figure either *Hurquar* or *Orgoth Vortai* should be our next step. Those two Constables were from *Hurquar*, but I don't know if they went back."

"No, I like *Orgoth Vortai*," Xiomber said. "Let's take it back to where it began. Is *Orgoth Vortai* going to be safe? That's the next question."

Morty nodded.

"No place is safe," Morty said. "But Omerlon's got no reason to like Maximus. Less if that's who did Damabiath."

But Morty liked the thought of *Orgoth Vortai* as well.

Knowing the Grace, they would see the whole thing as a giant piece of insane performance art.

But for the bombs going off, Morty would, too.

TIP

A KNOCK at the door brought Gareth's head up. He had been quietly reading criminal statutes, and making notes on a pad of paper as a cross-referenced index, comparing the *Accord of Souls* legal system to Earth Force. The table was covered with piles of paper and note cards, but he was almost done. After this, time to begin memorizing some of the more interesting details of the seventeen species that made up the *Accord*.

"Come in," he yelled.

The door was never locked. He had no reason to lock it as most of the people at this facility generally stayed well away from him anyway.

Oh, they were friendly enough, but all of them belonged to species that were within two or three percent of the absolute limits of genetic engineering and there was always some element of jealousy as to what he could do.

And nobody else could turn into a dragon, so he

had to be an alien of some sort, masquerading as a Vanir. Eventually, someone would probably figure it out. All hell would probably break loose when they did.

The door opened slowly. Talyarkinash poked her head in and looked around before opening it the rest of the way and stepping in.

"I forget that you need so little sleep as well," she began, a smile that went all the way to her ear tips lighting up her face. "I was afraid I would be waking you up."

Gareth rose and smiled back.

"Homework," he gestured to the stacks of paper on the table between them.

A thought struck him as he looked down.

"Did you modify my brain?" he asked suddenly. "This didn't used to be this easy."

People with fur on their face could hide a blush. But he had spent enough time around the Nari woman to see the subtle signs. The way her whiskers twitched back. Her ears turned a quarter rear as well. The pupils opened wider than necessary for the light in here.

"Maybe a little," she said in an off-hand way as she entered. "Maximus was already a genius, so I thought you could always use a bump."

"How much?" he pressed, sitting back down as clues and hints began to coalesce.

"There is a line, according to what Sarzynski told Morty and Xiomber," she offered, stepping fully into the room and closing the door behind her. "On the other side of that line, you get genius, but frequently human artists are also insane, according to his understanding of human history. To us, that is a relative concept, since all humans are completely deranged to begin with."

She said the last with a grin that brought a smile to Gareth's face as well. Nobody had worked as closely with any human as she had with him over the last six weeks. She was now the *Accord's* certifiable expert.

"You said on the other side of that line," Gareth prodded her.

"Correct," she agreed. "You were already well above average for humans, by your standards, but there was still space to bump you up further, so I did. Right now, you straddle that line, but that just means your memory is sharper and your reactions have improved some. Oh, and all your senses are sharper than before, but not so bad as to overwhelm you, but you already knew that."

"Thank you," he said. "I was beginning to wonder how I could memorize so much material, so quickly, but there was just too much I needed to know, so I come back here after dinner and read and take notes until after zero."

"I'm glad it has worked out," Talyarkinash admitted. "So much of what I was doing was guesswork, taking you and extrapolating along predicted lines to what I hoped were logical conclusions. And turning you into a dragon."

He grinned from ear to ear.

"Every kid wants to be a dragon, when they're about seven," he said. "Right after the dinosaur phase and before astronaut. It's a human thing."

"I see," she nodded and shrugged.

Being the best expert on humans they had didn't make her an expert on the species. Gareth was better for that, but nobody could bring themselves to fully trust him. He knew that.

Maybe Talyarkinash, but that was about it.

"You have news?" he asked, prompting her back from where he had derailed her.

Talyarkinash moved to the table and pulled the other chair. It was Nari-sized, so she could join him for tea or to chat.

"We've received orders to pack our personal gear," she said nervously. "Senior Constable Grodray is relocating us to *Orgoth Vortai*."

"Why there?" Gareth asked.

She shrugged meaningfully.

"Perhaps they have a tip?" she offered. "Maybe they just want someplace relatively used to strange things. You can't get much weirder than the homeworld of the Grace."

Gareth shrugged in turn.

"How soon until we leave?" he looked at his piles and began sorting them into things to keep and things to recycle.

"There will be a shuttle for us mid-day tomorrow," Talyarkinash said. "Around fifteen hours."

Gareth turned and looked at the closet door. It was closed, but he could have picked out every outfit in there blindfolded.

There wasn't much to begin with. Beyond two Constabulary uniforms, there was his Secret Agent/cowboy outfit that he had been wearing when

Marc captured him. A set of lovely robes that Morty had bought, but he had never worn. And his Sky Patrol uniform.

None of them fit him, being sized for the human he had been, once upon a time, but he wasn't about to lose them. Any of them.

At least in the future, laundry was a much easier task. Walk into the booth fully clothed and let all the various beams and radiations clean you and your clothes at the same time. Gareth had two more of Talyarkinash's special uniforms, designed to morph with him. One tunic was for normal duty, while the other was a touch fancier and would be for those weird, formal occasions where he was expected to be in dress uniform.

He hadn't been to anything like that yet, but supposed that he might have just graduated and be ready to become a Deputy Agent again.

Starting at the bottom was okay. He was a cop and there was work to be done.

"Thinking about your past?" Talyarkinash asked when he turned back to face her.

"My future, actually," he said. "The past is lost. I haven't made peace with that yet, but I'm working on it."

"You miss her?" she said. It was more of a statement, but it sounded enough like a question.

"Every day," Gareth sighed. "If it wasn't such an amazingly bad idea, I'd sneak back to Earth and bring her here with me. Have you turn her into a Vanir so we could live happily ever after. The Constabulary would never accept it, though. There are already too many humans here."

She wanted to say something. He could see it in her eyes, but she refrained. There wasn't much to say at that point. He could never go home, and he would probably end up in a cell, once he captured or killed Marc.

It would be apocalyptic, their final battle. Gareth had no doubts about that. Hopefully, he would prevail, and could bring peace to the *Accord of Souls*. Whether Marc would allow himself to be taken alive was another question.

Either way, the end of Marc Sarzynski's reign of terror would also be the end of Gareth's freedom. He wasn't sure how he felt about that, but duty was duty. Stop Marc first. Then deal with spending the rest of his days in prison as an illegal alien who was too dangerous to allow to roam free.

Rather than speak, Talyarkinash held out a hand. Gareth took it and held on.

It was nice to have friends, because they both knew whatever was coming was likely to get ugly, before it might ever get better.

INTO THE SHADOWS

"WE KNEW THEY WEREN'T THERE," Marc heard Zorge explain. "But, following orders, we planted a small bomb anyway and annihilated the place with fire."

Zorge paused at that point. When Marc turned to stare at him, the Nari spymaster was looking for the right words. Something that would get to the heart of the matter, without offending the crazy human boss who had cut such a bloody swathe across the *Accord*.

The group had taken over a small resort on the outskirts of the city of Uwethis, on *Kani*. It was about as far from the civilized core of the *Accord* as one could get and still have indoor plumbing, as the joke went. Planetary population still under a half billion souls, but a good mix of species in the city. And one of the lowest rates of cops to citizens in known space. A safe enough place to hide while he rebuilt the organization.

Marc relaxed on an overstuffed chair done in

green, while the Nari was on an equally-over-stuffed couch in gray and yellow squares. Hideous, but he wasn't an interior decorator.

"*Why?* you were wanting to ask?" Marc smiled as the pause stretched.

"Something like that, yes," Zorge replied defensively.

"They weren't there, but had been," Marc explained. "The criminal underground on *Churquark* isn't as well organized as *Zathus* had been. Not as powerful either, relying too much on corrupt politicians and mid-level folks to get by. They might have considered letting things slide."

"So bombing the place sends a message?" Zorge asked. "To whom?"

"Everyone," Marc actually felt a smile on his face. Those were rare, these days. "It tells those two that I can find them, and that I won't accept their apologies. It reminds the local underworld that anyone wanting to shelter the two lizardmen will be dealing with me, personally. It tells the Constabulary that things are more rotten than they think, so they'll concentrate more effort on *Churquark* than they had been."

"Net result, drive Morty and Xiomber off planet, right about the time the cops drop a ton of bricks on the place," Zorge concluded. "They escape the dragnet, and nobody else?"

"Exactly," Marc said. "Think of it as a shell game. Everyone will be looking on *Churquark*, where the marble is not hiding. I don't know where they'll go, but we've made the rest of the people around them unwelcoming, so they'll have no choice but to run. Eventually, we'll find them. Or the cops will."

"Won't they talk?" Zorge asked. "Tell the cops everything they know, trying to buy a reduced sentence?"

"Everything they know doesn't include what I'm up to now," Marc smiled. "You're still thinking defensively."

"And we're rebuilding, while bringing down all the other gangs," Zorge breathed. "But won't that make it harder for us, if they start bringing in honest politicians? Or clean up the local police departments?"

"For a while," Marc said. "I've been studying the *Accord's* history, and one thing is clear. The structure they built was never going to last forever. Too fragile. The Vanir might be all law-and-order as a rule, but their place at the top of the hierarchy of things tends to rub a lot of the other species the wrong way. And so you get an underclass that don't see how they can get ahead when the Vanir are so dominant."

"Which breeds resentment, and creates the conditions for the underworld to thrive," Zorge agreed.

"And I don't see that pattern changing," Marc said. "At least not for several more centuries. At some point, the Chaa might just have to come back and fix things if they want to go back to the old days, but I'm here now, and nobody's done anything about it, so either they don't see me as a threat, or, more likely, they don't care."

"And you plan to be around for that long still?"

"Correct," Marc said.

He studied the Nari closely, but the man didn't have any obvious qualms. Of course, without Maximus protecting him, the man would be a cell quickly enough. They were all in the chute now, and they knew it.

Victory or death.

Zorge shrugged.

"So I have my teams watching for all the key players," Zorge continued. "Grodray and Baker disappeared for three days last week, but they're back on *Hurquar* now, working to unravel everything there."

Marc nodded.

"My theory is that they went to visit Gareth Dankworth, wherever he had been hidden," Marc replied. "Now they're getting desperate enough to use him."

"Should we target him for anything?"

"No," Marc said firmly. "Just watch him for now. Perhaps he'll lead us to Morty and Xiomber. If he does, we'll sweep them all up, but I need better weapons, if I'm going to take on a star dragon."

"That's Maiair's department," Zorge said.

"Indeed," Marc agreed. "Anything else? Then send her in next."

"Yes, sir."

And the Nari spymaster was gone.

Marc looked around the room. Not bad, as resorts in the middle of nowhere went. Wood paneling on the walls made them feel small and intimate. Strange knick-knacks seemed to cover every free space on the abundant bookshelves, although he had no interest in ever reading the vast array of cozy mysteries and romances that the *Accord* writers seemed to generate on an annual basis.

He had a small front room with the couch, the overstuffed chair, and a writing hutch that could fold down. Down a short passageway was a tiny bathroom on the left, a kitchenette at the end, and a sleeping room barely big enough for the bed on the right. But this wasn't a place tourists stayed all day.

They were close to a variety of what Marc would have called nature preserves back on Earth. Places to hike and camp, all a short ride away. The resort had a kitchen and a small bar up in the main building, but Marc had arranged to rent the entire facility for a month. It was the off-season on *Kani*, not far past the middle of winter at this latitude, so the owner had made them a great deal, especially when Marc didn't need staff on hand for cooking and such.

He could have the place to himself for a while, cheap, and let his people work. Singles and doubles coming and going wouldn't excite any gossip with the locals. They had been given a cover story of a small religious group on a retreat, so they could be self-contained.

Let the storm blow over the *Accord* right now, while he was sheltered. The fundamental mechanics had not changed, so all Gareth and the Constables could do would be to imprison the current batch of criminals, until Marc could bend the new batch to his will.

It might take a decade, but Vanir were long-lived

folk to begin with, and he had plans for upgrading this body.

Emperor Marc. Not even Marc the First, as he planned to live as close to forever as medicine and genetics would allow, so he would give up the throne when it was taken from him in death, or when one of his sons finally impressed him enough to take over.

God/Emperor. Yes, that sounded more accurate.

A knock at the door, and then Maiair entered a moment later. Her crimson headcrest was carefully at half-mast. Unsure but firm and proud. Not challenging his authority, but not backing off of her own.

Good.

He had been afraid that the stress of the last month might have ground the Warreth woman down. Used her up. Broken her.

He could see he had been wrong.

"You wanted to see me?" she asked in a voice that found that perfect spot between subservient and sarcastic.

"Yes," he smiled at her, gesturing to the sofa for her to sit. Hopefully, she would be at ease.

Like Zorge, she was poised at the edge of the seat rather than putting her weight back.

"Things are beginning to move," Marc began. "Shortly, all of the enemy pieces will be on the table again, and we can begin our more complex gambits."

"What do I need to concentrate on?" she asked, her headcrest perking up some, fluffing a little as she grew more confident in the direction of the meeting.

"Gareth St. John Dankworth is a wild card,

Maiair," Marc said quietly. "Zorge has his people trying to get me information from the Constables, as to what his capabilities truly are, but without Liamssen's notes, we're only guessing. I need you to find me a competent geneticist that we own, or can turn."

"Kidnap?" she hazarded.

"No," Marc replied flatly. "I'll be putting my life in his hands, so I want one with a god complex and so much intellectual arrogance that he sees me as a challenge for his brilliance, rather than as an opportunity to destroy me in one shot."

"They come in flavors," she observed. "What kinds of upgrades were you needing for yourself? Liamssen was among the best as a generalist, and the rest are being prodded enough by the Constables enough to be looking over their shoulders constantly."

"I am bigger and stronger than most Vanir," Marc noted. "Smarter than just about all of them, as well. But Dankworth and the others didn't stop there. He can turn into a flipping dragon, for God's sake. I need something to counter that, but I'm not sure what, yet."

"Draco-form?" she asked carefully.

"This is a genetic change, Maiair," he replied. "If Dankworth ever had children with a Vanir woman, it would probably be a trait that was passed down. If the *Accord* isn't ready for humans, they really won't be able to deal with lycanthropic dragons. No, I'm looking to found a dynasty, so I need to get as close to immortality as we can get, which won't be that hard, but I want to be able to do something nobody else in the *Accord* can do."

"Which is?" she hesitated, sensing something that left her nervous.

More nervous than she already was.

"Breed with other species," Marc replied carefully, almost tenderly. "There's no reason all my children should be Vanir, Maiair."

She sucked a nearly-silent gasp and froze perfectly still, like a rabbit in the grass hearing an owl's cry.

Marc left the silence hanging. She had hinted at such things earlier, but she probably never realized that Marc Sarzynski was capable of going there intellectually. The various species of the *Accord of Souls* had been fixed in place by the Chaa when most of them were *Uplifted,* and the Vanir became *Those Left Behind.* They could marry and live happy lives, but never cross-breed.

Hell, most of them had different chromosome counts, so fertility was truly impossible.

But if he told a conference of geneticists that something was simply impossible, a few would stand up and challenge him. Those were the ones he wanted. Immortality wasn't a red flag they could look at on a readout. It had to be inferred from a host of indicators all being too healthy at the same time.

Perhaps one who would make him immortal, and a second who could help Marc create a whole series of ruling castes over the current species. He had been serious about bringing in a few humans and adding them in as dons and capos. And his own children would probably require fifty years before they were stable enough as a royal family.

But Marc was measuring time in millennia.

"You're sure?" she finally spoke.

Her headcrest had nearly collapsed, but now it had risen again. Puffed out feathers around her head had relaxed as the moment of shock passed.

"We have the opportunity to reshape the *Accord of Souls*, Maiair," Marc almost whispered. "I see no reason to limit things to the Vanir. The Warreth should have a chance to shine, as should the Nari and even the Grace. I'm less confident in some of the other species, but we can look. Can you find me the right doctor?"

He paused again. This was where things got tricky.

On the one hand, she knew he was going to create a ruling caste of humans, led by a royal family of heavily modified Vanir. On the other, he had just offered her the chance to place her own offspring into that level of power as well.

Permanently.

And the best part? All of his children would not be bound by the *Accord of Souls*, so he would have a permanent underclass of peons that were generally incapable of doing the kinds of violence necessary to stop him.

He would only have to worry about the humans he brought over, and his own children.

And Gareth St. John Dankworth.

COTTON CANDY SKIES

GARETH JUST COULDN'T WRAP his head around the color of the daytime sky overhead. Not quite as pink as cotton candy, but not so far down into orange as to be salmon-colored. It haunted him, but that had been the moment when he truly understood that he stood under alien skies. Looking up and not seeing blue.

Xiomber had explained it to him eventually. The weird bacteria and things that floated in the sky, plus a soft, constant haze of dust from the deserts on the continent of Mishalque. *Orgoth Vortai* had more land than *Earth*, only some forty percent being oceans, rather than the seventy-five percent back home. Heat made that desert largely uninhabitable, except by researchers who burrowed down into the rocks by day for coolness.

But he was back in *Londra* now. Gareth hadn't even known the name of the city as he was passing through it. One minute he had been at The Arsenal.

The next, he was in a park on the other side of town, headed to a tea shop…

"You have a very far-away look on your face, Dankworth," Eveth Baker said in a voice strong enough to jar him out of daydreams.

"Last time I was here, six weeks ago, I was on planet for all of about six hours," he replied. "Still completely trapped in culture shock and trying to figure out what the hell was going on."

"And it made that big of impression on you?" she asked. Her voice had lost some of the ragged anger that had been with her all day.

She started to walk, so Gareth fell into stride with her. It was weird, working with a female partner. Back home, the few Women's Auxiliaries of Earth Force were more secretaries and such, rather than agents. Although, come to think about it, Gareth could think of a few women he had known who could have done this job at least as well as him. Maybe better.

Here, he was the junior agent, but Baker was treating him like a peer, rather than a semi-feral animal she needed to keep on a tight leash.

Pippa, for example, could have done this. She had graduated third in her entire class from college, but couldn't go on to get an advanced degree because no reputable program would enroll her, so she was doing something like *Reading The Law* to do advanced stellar physics with her father. She could have certainly handled this.

He had been raised that way, but Gareth wasn't sure now why women were thought to be such frail, fragile creatures, to be protected at all costs. Eveth

Baker was one of the toughest people he had ever met.

"Dankworth?" Baker prodded.

He had fallen silent in thought.

"The city? Yes," he said, finding his way back to conversation. "Still culture shocking over all the things females do here as a matter of course, where back home they can't."

"That sounds stupid," Constable Baker decided.

Gareth shrugged. He really couldn't argue, having just spent the last six weeks surrounded by competent, capable females doing things that he had always thought of as a man's job.

"What's the next stop?" he asked instead.

They were dressed like cops today. Both in the steel-blue bodysuits with the bright blue ring over their hearts as a badge. Like always, she wasn't wearing the extra tunic over the top, but Gareth was trying to be the spit-and-polish rookie cop here, so he had everything exactly to regulation, including the white beret.

That also included a stun pistol like hers. Plus strict instructions from Eveth Baker never to draw it. He would probably do so automatically, if danger appeared, but he would argue with her over it afterwards.

She really meant in most situations, and he found that acceptable. They weren't going to find Marc Sarzynski while randomly checking bars and dives.

No, he was out here beating the bushes in order to drive the game towards Senior Constable Grodray. There would be no glory for Gareth Dankworth, but that was acceptable as well. The fewer people that knew he existed in the *Accord of Souls*, the better everything was likely to be.

"Here," Baker pointed to a building that had remained behind when the neighborhood was gentrified and redone at some point in the recent past.

The apartment towers behind him had a recent feel to them, like a row of houses had been leveled and a massive stack of flats with a giant picture of a rooster on the side put in instead, with two stories of retail and office space at the bottom.

This was a solitary building in front of them. One story tall. Sitting on a corner facing the main street they were on as well as the side. The outside walls were wood, with neon signs for things Gareth presumed were local beers. It had that kind of feel to it.

Weirdly, the front door was Dutch. The top half was open, and the whole sat recessed at a forty-five degree angle, facing the center of the intersection rather than either street. Baker unlatched the bottom half and pushed it in.

Gareth followed her into a space that managed to carefully surf that line between upscale restaurant and neighborhood dive bar. Four booths ran down the right hand wall, with a hallway indicating restrooms beyond.

On the left, high and low tables filled the bulk of the space. Maybe forty of them, all told, with a waist-high, wrought-iron fence separating the space from a bar that ran halfway across the back wall. A window and a door beside the bar showed a kitchen, but

Gareth could already tell that from the smells. Outside had been nice, a smell like a Sunday afternoon grilling.

Inside, the smells trebled. Gareth's stomach rumbled in anticipation of the meat and yummies to be had here.

Three people sat at the bar, their backs to he and Baker as they came in. A Grace bartender watched them from under hooded eyes and restive coils, but gestured to the room.

"Anywhere you like," he called in a voice that was just about as friendly as he was required to be to cops walking in in the middle of the afternoon.

Baker led him to one of the booths and slid in, tapping the other side to indicate where he should go. He ended up with his back to the front door, the bar on his left, and the hallway in front of him, over her shoulder.

The menus were meat. It came grilled, fried, barbequed, sous vide, and probably tartar. Gareth could recognize about half of the animals that were the source by now. Vegetables came grilled as a side, or possibly in a salad for someone that had been dragged along kicking and screaming by hungry carnivores.

Baker studied the menu, while Gareth looked over at the inhabitants.

The Grace woman on the closest end of the bar looked over as they sat, blanched, and quickly paid her bill and vanished. A Borren drunk at the other end leaned back enough to look over and then went back to his beer. Or whatever it was in his glass.

The man in the middle was a species Gareth had never met before, though he had studied them. Th'Tarni.

They reminded Gareth of wood elves, as portrayed in stories. A little over five feet tall, with a dusky skin that wasn't gray and wasn't brown and wasn't smoke, but somewhere in the middle of all three. Back home, he might have belonged to the negro subgroup, based on the color of his skin and his flat nose. They weren't that common in Earth Force Sky Patrol, so Gareth had never really interacted with them.

This man's eyes were the most fascinating. They didn't have an iris and pupil, like most species, but simply a transparent orb for an eyeball, lit from within with a shy, baby-blue light that stood out against the gray-brown skin. Similar dots of color on his skin were freckles, or the roots of his hair. That same hair faded to gray and then black quickly, but always had some of the cerulean along all edges, like it was part of a neon sign.

The ears were pointed, like Gareth's were now, but instead of going straight up, this man's flowed backwards and then rose to points nearly even with the back of his skull. They also glowed with the same internal light.

It was like the man was made of light and given a shell. Or maybe he was a gigantic lightning bug given human form by the Chaa.

The man turned as he watched and glared at Gareth, almost challenging. Gareth realized he was staring and quickly turned his head down to study the menu again, blushing furiously.

He thought he heard a snicker come from Baker, but couldn't be sure and wasn't going to ask.

Suddenly, music engulfed the room. Gareth glanced over and the bartender was responsible. Probably to keep conversations more private. Maybe it was just late enough in the day that this was when he normally turned the jukebox on.

And pigs might fly.

The bartender meandered over, making it clear from his stance that he was serving them because they had walked in and had badges, and not because he liked their kind in his joint.

"What'll it be?" he called over the music in a rasp that bordered on rude.

Gareth checked the small section at the bottom of the drinks menu. Seventy-three kinds of beer and hard cider. Eight things without. Half of those were mixers in hard drinks.

"Cola," he said simply.

"Anything in it?" the man almost sneered.

Gareth fixed him with a hard stare.

"Ice," he said in a growling tone.

The Grace blinked and recoiled, ever so slightly.

Two can play at that game, buddy.

"Coffee," Baker added. "Hot and black. Preferable strong enough to stand a knife up in it."

"See what I can do," the Grace man moved away quickly.

Like they were toxic to his physical being, not just his state of mind.

"We eating?" Gareth asked quietly, letting the music cover his tones. "And is it safe to eat here?"

Baker actually let go of her hard-ass persona long enough to give him a genuine smile.

"Very safe," she said in a similar, quiet voice. "Best bacon on the planet, as far as I'm concerned. And don't let Ray's demeanor fool you. He's been a source for me for years. This is all just an act, so feel free to bad cop him as much as you think he deserves."

"Roger that," Gareth acknowledged.

The bartender, Ray apparently, returned a few minutes later with a brown-black glass for Gareth, *with ice*, and a mug of coffee and additives for Baker. She ordered a pulled pork sandwich and a plate-of-bacon sampler. Gareth got a mac and cheese with all the bacon added it.

Seriously, they had bacon made from three different kinds of animals. None of them were pigs. How weird was that?

About the time that more customers started to wander in, the Th'Tarni man paid his bill. He fixed Gareth with a long, appraising stare, and then sauntered out of the room like the King of Brooklyn, robes swishing to show off elaborate embroideries over the front and sleeves. Gareth decided the man needed a small hat, maybe a kufi or a chador, to make the outfit perfect, but maybe the colorful hair didn't like a lid.

It must be happy hour, Gareth decided. By the time food was delivered, nearly a quarter of the tables in here suddenly had custom, and a Vanir waitress had come on duty.

She wasn't as tough-looking as Baker, nor all that attractive as a woman. Tall and kind dumpy, with too many tattoos visible and a paunch around the middle. She did had a smile for him, every time she caught him looking over, though.

The food was absolutely fantastic. Nothing like what his Mom would have cooked, but his mother wasn't that good of a cook, preferring to pull something out of the freezer and either toss it into the stove or the microwave-emitter. Or better, when Gareth had finally gotten old enough, to have him do it himself.

He looked down and considered licking the bowl clean but his tongue wasn't long enough. If he had gotten any bread, this would have been the time to smear it and pick up any cheese sauce left.

Baker was watching him with mirthful eyes when he looked up, rather at odds with how she had been for the last three days. Gareth studied her carefully, like she was about to ask him a final exam question that counted for twenty-five percent of his grade.

"You're very quiet for a rookie," she observed.

"I'm only a rookie in your department, Baker," he said sincerely. "I've been doing this for almost eight years in mine. Plus, I don't want to screw up your investigation, so I'm trying to listen and learn."

She nodded slowly. The grin hadn't left her eyes, even as the rest of her face fell into seriousness.

The bartender, Ray, approached in his casual, unruffled-by-cops saunter, and placed a small, black binder on the table with a "Whenever you're ready," before he fled back to the bar.

Baker pulled out her wallet from a thigh pouch, extracting a credit card plus something else. Gareth thought he saw her palm a piece of paper and stick it into the binder with her card, closing it and laying it flat on the edge of the table.

Gareth concentrated on what was left of his cola, the music, and the crowd. He could tell the place had gentrified and done so fairly recently. A young Nari woman walked in and one point and asked about a job, but Ray explained that everybody loved this place so much that nobody ever quit. She left, but Gareth could tell she was from the old neighborhood, not the place that it was turning into.

Others at various tables had the feel of businessmen out for a late meeting happy hour beer, or an early dinner before heading out for a night on the town.

Ray came back and retrieved the binder. Gareth thought he detected a ghost of a nod between Ray and Baker, but it might have been his imagination.

Baker didn't say anything, just kept watching over his shoulder.

A few minutes later, Ray emerged from the back and slid the binder in front of Baker, again retreating, almost disdainfully, rather than make small talk.

Baker opened it, fiddled around with the papers inside, and then signed one. Again, Gareth thought he saw her palm a folded piece of paper, but she slid out of the booth quickly and stood before he could ask her about it.

Gareth joined her. In addition to being a cop in this joint, he and Baker were the only two Vanir, other than the waitress. Gareth almost felt like he was walking in a middle school lunch hall, being a head or two taller than almost everyone else.

It might have been his imagination, but there seemed to be a small bubble of silence that rippled along with them as they exited. Each table they had passed had seemed to quiet down for a beat, perhaps as the occupants looked over, before it picked up again.

Back out on the street, Baker retraced her steps with a jaunty stride. Gareth had to stretch his legs just to keep up with her, which was another strange feeling.

"You done good in there, Dankworth," she said after they had gotten two blocks away. "Professional without looking like a rookie. Not letting anything throw you off. Nicely done."

"Why was *Tornado* so important?" he asked, referring to the restaurant behind them.

"Ray, the bartender?" she said. "He owns it, and has for a long time, but it has always been something of an underworld hangout. Neutral ground. Everyone minds their manners in there, and nobody says anything. Probably a quarter of the people in there with us had criminal records, possibly active warrants."

"And you let a place like that exist?" Gareth was aghast.

"Better the devil you know," she replied carefully. "Plus, Ray provides a forum where enemies can meet and work things out. Better than bloodshed. Even cops can have conversations with criminals in there, as long as nobody raids the place."

"What would happen if they got raided?" Gareth asked.

This was so far outside his normal expectations of law enforcement that he couldn't wrap his head around it.

"Everybody would make common cause on the person responsible," she said in a serious voice. "That includes the Constabulary helping the local dons take someone down. It's not the best arrangement, but it keeps a lid on things, at least until we can do more to get rid of the rotten elements in society. That's where you come in."

"Me?" he asked, almost faltering in his stride.

"You," she agreed. "When those two Yuudixtl brought you here, they started a chain of events. Sarzynski overplayed his hand and we nearly broke his organization. Right now, he's spending more time fighting with the underworld than with us. More thugs have been arrested in the last month than the previous year. Crooked prosecutors are suddenly having to go to court because of the increased visibility, and bad guys are going to jail rather than getting off on technicalities and witnesses refusing to cooperate."

"Huh," Gareth replied. "I've been off training and studying, so I didn't see any of this."

"Yes," she said. "We've intentionally kept you in the dark up until now. But Grodray wants you visible now. Being seen with me. Word will get around."

"Who are we looking for?" Gareth said.

Baker stopped walking now and pulled out her comm. She called an auto-taxi and turned to him.

"Anybody that panics when they see you," she said with a predatory smile. "You don't exist, so you're just another Vanir cop. But if they know anything different, I want to put them in a small room and sweat them."

"Okay," Gareth said as the car landed and the door opened.

He followed her inside and buckled his belt.

"And that note you passed Ray?" he continued.

That got him another smile. Gareth wasn't sure he was a ready for an Eveth Baker who smiled a lot.

"I told him I wanted a name," she said, pulling the paper out.

She unfolded it and read it quickly, nodding to herself.

"Now the fun begins," she smiled at him.

Gareth wondered if a shark smiled like that, right before he took a bite out of your leg.

"What's next?" he asked.

"Now we put your superpower to work," she replied.

Gareth really didn't like the sound of that.

POSSIBILITIES

SHE FOUND the closed door intimidating, but Talyarkinash didn't let that stop her. It was unlocked she found, so she pushed it in and entered the room.

From the outside, this was just another tower in Londra, the art capital of *Orgoth Vortai*. And that was all the Grace really cared about. Art.

The actual capital city, where politics got done, was Burich, but that was a sleepy, college town two hundred kilometers up the Temin River. All the action was in Londra, or possibly down in Xarxe, the port city down on the delta where so many musicians had gathered together.

Talyarkinash preferred Londra. Living in a tower with a mix of flats and offices, depending on the floor and the lift tube you used. There was supposedly an indoor arcade filled with shops and restaurants, taking up the first two floors above ground and three below, but she had never seen it.

She was still in police custody, even if everyone

was too polite to call her a prisoner to her face. She did not leave this floor without an armed escort, so she could call it what it was.

The room she entered was bland and meaningless. That took significant work on the homeworld of the Grace, since they saw any blank wall as an invitation and excuse to commit art. Someone had consciously undone this room. White walls greeted her, with pedestrian watercolor pictures on two walls, plus a large picture window looking out over the rest of the city. Brown carpets as bland as the walls under her feet.

Senior Constable Jackeith Grodray was already seated across from her, with a stack of folders off to one side. The small room was dominated by a cherry-oak table, Vanir-sized, that worked as either a desk or a conference table for a small group. Another Vanir, this one a woman, was seated on Grodray's right.

Like him, she wore the generic uniform of the Constabulary. They didn't wear names or ranks indicators of any kind, unlike most of the police departments she had ever known, so Talyarkinash had no way of identifying the woman's place in things, except by age.

She had been skinnier when she was younger, that much was obvious, but the Vanir woman was much older now. Not plump, but not the lean huntress the younger version had obviously been. More senior. Possibly into her eighth or tenth decade. Dark hair was now streaked with silver and white. The flesh of her neck was slack, and her eyes and forehead were a maze of wrinkles that Talyarkinash suspected led one to the minotaur, rather than the treasure.

Grodray rose as Talyarkinash closed the door carefully.

"Dr. Talyarkinash Liamssen, this is Dr. Dalton Fitzroy," Grodray introduced the woman. "Prime Investigator with an emphasis on biology and genetics."

Indeed? Talyarkinash had never heard of a Constable with advanced degrees in those sorts of things, but considering the uses to which they were generally put, the woman most likely would have been undercover. Or recruited as a cop later. Or the Constabulary had a secret university where only cops were trained. She made a note to inquire at some point.

Talyarkinash had spent the last decade in her lab ignoring the outside world, getting filthy, stinking rich. Some of it was still hidden away, in places that might not have been discovered yet. Cops like Grodray had already taken the rest of her life apart and confiscated most of her ill-gotten gains.

Fitzroy rose and held out a hand.

"Dr. Liamssen," she said in a pleasant, alto voice.

"Dr. Fitzroy," Talyarkinash replied, shaking the hand.

The woman was almost as tall as Grodray, standing. Talyarkinash willed herself to stillness, expecting the woman to show off her strength by squeezing, but she didn't.

"Please, be seated," Grodray said, putting deed to word.

Talyarkinash found that they had given her a seat that could telescope up enough to make the Vanir-height table comfortable, as long as she didn't mind her feet swinging in the air.

Fitzroy's eyes bored into her as Talyarkinash watched.

"I have studied your work extensively, Dr. Liamssen," the woman cop began suddenly. "It is a pleasure to finally meet you in the flesh."

The tone was nice enough, but Talyarkinash had a feeling that there were layers of cop ugliness concealed underneath. How long had they been trying to pin something on her and failing? How many of her former patients had they found? Or only suspected?

So many of her files had been carefully hidden away and encrypted, but that was before she became a ward of the state and turned them and the decryption key over to Grodray.

Which only made it funnier, since the crime that finally got her taken down might be the most honest thing she had ever done.

"You have me at a disadvantage, then," Talyarkinash replied. "How may I be of service?"

"I would like to talk about Gareth Dankworth," the older cop began. "And then the one known these days as Maximus."

Talyarkinash nodded. As she suspected when she opened the door. She was the expert right now, but the *Accord of Souls*, and very specifically the Constabulary, needed more experts on humans.

It was entirely possible that they would never

cram that djinn back into the bottle, three wishes or not.

"You've reviewed my report on Gareth?" she asked carefully. "Both the baseline values and the upgrades?"

"I have," Fitzroy replied. "But those were written for the lay officer. The men and women who do not have a deep understanding of species genetics. Jackeith Grodray, for example."

Talyarkinash nodded again. Entirely accurate, as that was exactly what he had asked her to produce.

"You wish to understand the implications of the baseline?" Talyarkinash hazarded a guess.

"I do," the woman said. "Unlike most of the Constabulary, I have studied humans in great detail, something that brought me out of retirement six months ago when it was feared that a human had escaped into the *Accord of Souls*. Before anyone knew the truth."

"That one Marc Sarzynski, AKA *Maximus*, was born a human on Earth, and illegally transported to *Zathus*," Talyarkinash acknowledged. "Before being illegally upgraded by myself and the two Yuudixtl scientists known as Morty and Xiomber, no known last names. How well do you understand humans?"

"At one point, research was done to determine if the *Accord of Souls* should send an agent to Earth to introduce a virus that would completely eliminate the species while not destroying other life forms," Fitzroy answered in a calm, bland voice.

Talyarkinash gasped and felt her blood drain to her stomach. Wipe out humans? Just like that?

But it also made a cruel sense. They were not part of the *Accord of Souls*. They were not part of the psionic collective, not bound by non-violence. Such a thing was monstrous, but at the same time logical. And practical, if humans were that dangerous a species.

"And you did the research?" Talyarkinash guessed.

"I did," Fitzroy smiled grimly.

Talyarkinash turned to Grodray with an angry face.

"I am never going to see the light of day again, am I?" she hissed. "I know too much to even see the inside of a prison cell, if you decided you no longer needed me?"

"On the contrary, Talyarkinash Liamssen," Grodray smiled back grimly, still nodding in acknowledgement. "While that was exactly the case five weeks ago, I have had agents paying close attention to your every word and action since then. You are never without some level of surveillance. And you never will be. Make no mistake there. Yes, you know too much. But you have also thrown yourself whole-heartedly into trying to undo the mistakes you had made. Into making Gareth into the monster he became, because you and the other two believed that it might be the only way to save the *Accord* from utter destruction. You have provided the records we needed to arrest more than fifty prominent criminals that you had previously modified to let them escape justice. Those factors also weigh in your favor."

Huh.

"Knowledge is dangerous, Dr. Liamssen," Fitzroy spoke up. "But heart and soul matter. Gareth Dankworth has proven himself to be even more willing than you to face whatever consequences arise, whatever sacrifices he must make. That has impressed even the most surly agents, such as myself."

Talyarkinash kept her eyes on Grodray, aiming her sensitive nose at the messages he was giving off, even unconsciously.

"So I'm not to be just drained like a lemon and tossed onto the ash heap of history?" Talyarkinash snarked.

"According to my cohort," Grodray gestured to Fitzroy, "you might be the single most capable geneticist in the *Accord of Souls* right now. It would be the utter heights of folly not to take advantage of those skills. We have Gareth on our side. They have a rogue in Marc Sarzynski. Dalton Fitzroy is here because we may need more."

"More?"

"How much more capability could we engineer into Gareth?" Fitzroy asked in a serious, scholarly voice. "Should we consider recruiting a second Sky Force officer?"

Talyarkinash laughed before she could smother it or cover her mouth.

"If you have studied baseline humans, how would you rank Gareth Dankworth on their scale?" Talyarkinash asked the older woman.

"In the top one percent physically." Fitzroy replied. "In the top four percent mentally. I've actually been able to study his records from Earth Force, to compare them to his current form."

"How?" Talyarkinash gasped. "No. Don't tell me. It's obvious you must have spies and systems in place, if you need to keep this close of a track on them. Gareth was using fourteen percent of his genetic capabilities as a human, the moment before I hit him with the six transformation virus injections. Marc Sarzynski, according to Gareth, was so close to him in all ways as to be identical, save for hair color and ethical standards."

"Fourteen?" It was Grodray's turn to gasp. "Where did you take him to?"

"Roughly thirty-one percent," Talyarkinash replied. "I haven't been given access to the quality of lab I had at home, or my full notes, to nail it down closer than that. Gareth is now the strongest, fastest, and toughest Vanir you will probably ever meet, excepting only Sarzynski. Both are in the top one hundred for intelligence, but Maximus has an edge there because I purposefully kept Gareth on this side of a line that frequently risks significant mental instability in humans."

"What about the dragon?" Fitzroy asked, leaning forward and staring intently.

"Gareth's idea," she admitted. "He wanted something that apparently instills fear in humans, and would probably do the same in the *Accord of Souls*. He wanted a symbol. So the transformation makes him hexapodal and grants him scales as a layer of dermal armor. The costume I built for him uses his own DNA as a signature, so that it will become part of the transformation and undo later."

"He can fly and breath fire," Fitzroy noted. "What are the limitations there?"

"I don't know," Talyarkinash admitted with an honest shrug.

"Why not?" Grodray leaned into the conversation. "How is that possible?"

"Gareth's abilities tap into a vast, unconscious pool of human psionic energy," Talyarkinash said. "I gave him the power to reshape himself as he needed, but I can no more explain how it works than you could describe blue to a man born blind, Constable. She might be a better expert there."

"Fitzroy?"

It was Talyarkinash's turn to sit back and watch. And it was fascinating, watching the woman pick and choose her words carefully.

"I suspect Liamssen speaks the bald truth, Jack," she said.

Talyarkinash had never heard the man called by the diminutive of his first name, which told her how close these two must have worked in the past. Teacher and pupil?

"Gareth once told me his limitations might be his imagination," Talyarkinash offered. It was like tossing gasoline onto a fire, to watch the two of them flinch.

"And Maximus?" Grodray asked.

"The same," she concluded. "Except that all I did was modify him into a top of the line Vanir physically. Morty and Xiomber did the mental work, so you'll have to ask, if you can locate them. I went well beyond the basics with Gareth. There's no reason another geneticist worth her egg couldn't do the same."

Grodray reached out a hand and opened the forgotten files, flipping through it until he found the page he wanted.

"Both you and Gareth have referred to the form as a Star Dragon," Grodray asked carefully. "What does that mean?"

"I used his terminology, Grodray," Talyarkinash replied. "But the basic form of the dragon could survive in space, at least as long as he could hold his breath, which we have not tested extensively. And fly there, if I understand things correctly. We haven't yet tested that either."

"Fly? In space?" Fitzroy asked. "How?"

"Again, the power is psionic, and not physical," Talyarkinash said. "Those wings could not lift his mass, nor carry it to those speeds, using simply physics. He does it, himself."

"And we have not tested it?" Grodray probed.

"We have not," she smiled. "He and I have been in custody since the moment his powers manifested."

"Huh," was all the man said.

Abruptly, he folded up his notes, gathered the folders in his hand, and stood.

"I will leave you two to talk, then," he said. "You'll both nerd out so quickly that I would become lost, but I look forward to talking to both of you tomorrow and learning your conclusions."

He left with a nod and Talyarkinash found herself alone with the older cop. This woman was still at least as dangerous right now as Eveth Baker had ever been on her best day, even as old as she was.

But Talyarkinash was here to save the galaxy, as weird as that would have seemed to her six months ago.

"What would you like to know?" she asked the woman.

HABERDASHER

GARETH RECOGNIZED the type of room, but this wasn't the same one he had visited with Morty and Xiomber. That had been a tower on the other side of town, if he remembered the layout of the streets correctly. It had all been culture shock at the time, and then meeting Keelee and getting tasted by a Grace for the first time.

He still shivered at that memory. Grace were weird, with tentacles instead of hair and vertically-slitted eyes, like a Nari, but otherwise could pass as a human, if they wore a hood.

But those tentacles…

What must it be like to be able to smell, taste, and touch with dozens of acutely-sensitive fingers at the same time? No wonder they all seemed to grow up to be artists, to live in a world that rich with sensory input.

Gareth had followed Baker into the room. It was big. Twenty meters on a side, with five meter ceilings, which was rare, even for Vanir offices. Two sofas on one side. A triple-mirror on the other.

This only differed from Jorghen's shop in that there was an desk with a computer console making the third point of a triangle. And a young Grace officer operating it. He looked up with a smile as they entered.

"Constable Baker," he nodded. "What can I do for you today?"

"Explorer Dankworth needs to go undercover, here in Londra," she said, gesturing for Gareth to walk closer to the man. "I need him to look like a mid-range punk, capable of fitting in with a party crowd while still looking like a tough guy. He'll be armed, so put an ankle holster into the mix."

"Fop or grinder?" the man asked, losing Gareth in the process. "Londra's nightlife is running down those two paths, this year. By next year, historical reenactments will be the rage, according to the fashion designers I'm in touch with."

Baker surprised Gareth by turning to study him, green eyes squinted in appraisal.

"Let's go grinder, right now," she replied. "But keep his measurements in the system in case we need to kick him out a second outfit on the fly."

"Will do," the Grace officer said. "Explorer, if you could move to the scanners?"

Gareth complied. Unlike Joghen's system, this one didn't have the light at the top that apparently looked inside his brain.

Gareth stopped and turned to the officer.

"Last time, there was a light," he said, rapping on the top of the center mirror. "Right here."

"You've done this before?" Baker was suddenly standing right there. "Been hard scanned for a new outfit? Where?"

"Here in Londra," Gareth said. "When we passed through *Orgoth Vortai* on the way to *Hurquar*. I thought I included that in my report?"

"You did," she nodded. "But I didn't realize that it had brain-scanned you fully."

"Is that a problem?" Gareth asked. "He pulled the outfit I wanted out of my subconscious."

"Do you remember the name of the place?" she pressed. "The name of the tailor?"

"Jorghen," Gareth said. "Last name unknown. Never saw him, as his console was in a different room and we talked over the house comm. Tower somewhere on the south side of town."

"Interesting," she said, reaching for her comm. "You get done and I'll talk to Grodray. Somebody might need to have a chat with this tailor."

Gareth nodded, a little lost, and turned back to the mirrors. He stood perfectly still as the other agent worked his controls, until there was an image of Gareth in all three screens. Instead of steel-blue, he was wearing mostly black, highlighted with emerald green.

Black, shiny, leather boots came up almost to his knees, done with green laces. Knickerbocker shorts met them in the middle over black socks, the pants baggy but not jodhpurs in cut. These used a black and green tartan pattern with a little gold thrown in.

Looking close, the fabric appeared to be a really nice wool, like a Scottish Laird might have worn.

The jacket was a blazer, sort of, except it had poofy patch pockets attached to the front instead of them being inside slits. Three buttons covered the front with a narrow lapel, but only the middle button was hooked. Instead of a dress shirt with a tie, he was wearing a black, knit pullover that tucked into the pants behind a brown, leather belt.

"Where's the holster go?" Baker asked abruptly, bringing Gareth back to the job at hand.

"Tucked into the bottom of the shorts," the Grace replied. "Accessible via the clasp that hold the knee hitch closed and generally concealed by the pleat and gather on the thighs. Are you right handed or left, Dankworth?"

"Right," he said, watching the Grace type something into the keyboard.

Gareth stopped himself from speaking. If this was a grinder, what must a fop look like? He had been expecting leather with chrome spikes, or something equally outrageous. This was almost something he could take golfing, if he could get the man to add threads for spikes to the bottom of the boots.

And he looked good.

But the best part was the new beret. It was huge, almost a tam-o-shanter in size, done in a coarse, black wool, with a gold medallion on the left side and a pair of feathers poking up that looked like they came from Stellar's Jays, bright, fierce blue.

"You like?" Baker asked, suddenly standing right next to him.

"I do," Gareth replied honestly. "Rugged but distinguished. I could wear that outfit many places without being self-conscious."

"Good," she smiled wickedly. "Because you're going to be bait."

Gareth suppressed a shudder at the way her voice sounded.

But who ever asked the worm how he felt?

ON THE RUN

"THOUGHTS?" Morty asked as the auto-taxi deposited them on the sidewalk and bounced back into the sky.

"We stay away from any spot where we took Gareth," Xiomber said. "Past that, we need a roof and I've got the munchies."

Morty nodded. Jorghen hadn't been his favorite tailor in Londra, but he had needed to keep Gareth's scent away from the woman who normally dressed him and his brother. He could imagine what it would have been like introducing her to Gareth.

And he would miss his favorite tea house, but the poor girl who had waited on them had probably been utterly traumatized by the time the cops got done with her. Seeing them again would likely bring it all back in a screaming flash that would end up with he and his egg-brother under arrest.

"Right," Morty said, turning right and heading east down the street. Downtown Londra was commercial, but there were all sorts of places on the east end that got deep into the Bohemian side of things. Just the place for a couple of renegade physicists to hide.

A bus dropped them at the edge of a park. The weather was passable nice today. Just warm enough that people were outside, but not warm enough to encourage the kinds of nude debauchery Morty had seen around here in the middle of summer.

Still, his favorite hot dog stand was doing a brisk business. He got five, figuring Xiomber would stop at two, like he normally did, and they'd have to hit the pastry shop on the far side of the park afterwards, as always. The coffee was bitter dark, but Stanz didn't like tea and Morty didn't want to stand in line for any of the other shops or stands.

They ended up not far from the water fountain, leaned back against a couple of rocks in a bushy area with a good view of the ball fields and generally out of sight. The fountain was off and the fields were abandoned right now, but both would change within a week or three.

They ate in silence, watching the few students studying and a couple of young mothers with strollers, but the park was amazingly empty. Just the way Morty liked it. So much harder for someone to sneak up on them.

Morty checked his watch as a private sedan landed clear across the way. Omerlon's people might be cut-rate punks, but they did understand punctuality. Three people piled out, two Grace and a

Warreth, and started across the field, leaving the vehicle and the driver over in the parking lot.

From their seats, it would be almost impossible for the guys coming to spot them, which was how Morty preferred it. Smuggling themselves across the galaxy was enough of a pain in the tail. Trying to get guns from a reputable fence at the same time was too much.

Plus, Omerlon didn't have any reason to hate them, as far as Morty knew. Nobody outside Sarzynski's gang even knew the new boss had been human once, not counting the cops, let alone knew that he and his egg-brother had been responsible for it. Better for everyone to keep it that way.

Nope, hopefully this was just a job interview, and they could settle in and do nice, simple, criminal things for the folks around here for a while, at least until he or Xiomber figured out a way to turn themselves into the Constables, or somebody actually managed to take Maximus down and they might be safe.

That happened, and Morty could see retiring to a nice desert somewhere, living off the ill-gotten gains of a disreputable life of crime without having to look over his shoulder constantly for assassins.

The two Grace thugs pulled up short and took up a spot off to one side. Visible, but not close enough to listen. The Warreth moved to the edge of the fountain and sat.

Morty turned to Xiomber.

"Last chance to change your mind," he said.

"Oh, hell no it isn't," Xiomber chirped. "I got lots

of chances to sell your stupid ass down the line and set myself up as a king."

Morty smiled.

"You aren't rich enough to buy the right babes, Xiomber," he sneered merrily. "Best you could do it rent them by the hour."

"And they'll still charge me half what they would you," Xiomber countered. "Let's do this. The dogs were good, but I want a turnover now."

Morty shrugged and rose. He emerged from the bushes first, with Xiomber close behind. Like the Warreth, they were wearing light jackets and heavy dungarees today, but everyone kept hands in the open, like polite thugs meeting in public.

"You Xiomber?" the Warreth asked as they got to speaking distance.

"Nope. Morty," he said, pointing over his shoulder. "That's Xiomber. You Danzeekar?"

"Correct," the Warreth replied.

The two Grace appeared to relax a little, turning each a little sideways to make sure nobody else suddenly decided to join this shindig, like, say, cops. Or assassins.

Morty had no doubts that all three were armed, but that was just part of the game these days.

He walked close enough to talk, but didn't feel like climbing up on the bench.

"So we're out of work and looking," Morty said.

"That's the message I got," Danzeekar replied. "Why is that?"

"Because Maximus is nuts and getting worse," Morty snapped. "Turning into a killer. Smart money's getting out now, while all the parts are still attached."

"So, free agents?" the Warreth asked haughtily.

"It's you or the cops, pretty boy," Morty sneered. "Nobody else has enough moxie to keep us safe from assassins. You need a couple of high-end physicists in the organization?"

"Rumors say that you two also do genetic work," the birdman observed in a neutral voice. "That true?"

"Yup," Morty smiled. "We did some of the upgrades on Maximus, along with Talyarkinash Liamssen."

"What kinds of upgrades?"

The beak was pointed this way now. Morty smiled as the headcrest popped up to full extension. He had the guy's attention and interest, finally. Dumb-ass punk.

"That's above your pay grade, pal," Morty said. "And sure as hell not something to talk about in the middle of a park in the middle of the day, *capiche*?"

"So you want to come in from the cold?" Danzeekar said. "Just like that?"

"We got information your boss will find interesting," Morty said. "Plus our skills and experience. You make us a good offer on salary and benefits, and we can do a deal. You empowered to negotiate at that level, or should we talk to the big guy?"

Morty held his breath while the Warreth considered. They really didn't have a lot of leverage, but Omerlon's folks wouldn't know how hard he was bluffing.

Hopefully.

And wouldn't call his bluff, either, because most of this was bluff.

"You got bonafides?" the man asked.

Bingo.

Morty nearly laughed out loud. Pretty boy was just a messenger, sure, but high enough ranking to dicker. Bonafides were secrets presented in good faith. That first taste of the cake before you bought the rest.

"Yeah," Morty said as he stuffed his hands into his front pockets. "We upgraded Maximus to a full genius intelligence level as part of the other things we did to him. Liamssen wasn't involved in that part."

"How the hell did you do that?" Danzeekar was shocked. "He's Vanir. They're already about as fixed as you can get."

Morty just smiled. Kinda rocked back and forth with his hands in his front pockets. Not *quite* mocking the guy.

"Oh, and the only other person who knows any of what we did?" he continued. "Talyarkinash Liamssen? She's in Constabulary custody, and has been for several weeks. I imagine, from my own sources, that she's spilled everything she knows. You saw how fast *Hurquar* has been dismantled in the last month, right? Wanna talk yet?"

"Yeah," the Warreth's headcrest bobbed three times. "You got a number we can reach you? Boss will want a sit-down after I talk to him."

"Nope," Morty said. "You leave a message with Stanz, the hot dog vendor. He's an old comrade of ours. I'll check in with him later and see where you'd like to meet. Dinner at an expensive joint, reasonably public, would do nicely."

Morty turned and walked back into the bushes. Xiomber was kinda crab-walking, to keep an eye on the Grace, but they made it to cover.

There was a little creek tucked in down there. Morty led his partner to it and skittered along the shore as fast as his stubby legs would allow.

When they emerged from the park ten minutes later, that sedan was gone, so Morty picked a side street with some traffic and headed north, Xiomber walking about forty meters behind so they didn't appear to be together, to a watcher looking for a pair of Yuudixtl males.

They settled into the pastry shop for turnovers and more coffee. Better, but still not tea.

"Think they'll go for it?" Xiomber asked around a mouthful of blueberry jam threatening to run down his front.

"Hope so," Morty replied. "They really are our last chance. After that, we either have to go straight, or go to the cops."

LIFEBLOOD OF THE GRACE

GARETH CLOSED the book and placed it atop a pile of three others on the sidetable next to his comfy reading chair. Two days and four books on the topic wasn't going to make him an expert on art, but he could at least have a reasonable conversation at the event without looking like a complete fool.

Plus Grodray had brought in an older man, a Grace of some note as an art historian, to prep him for tonight. Apparently, the older a Grace got, the longer their tentacles grew, so he must have been ancient, since some of his had come down to nearly his waist when they hung still.

And he knew everyone that was going to be at the show. This was *Orgoth Vortai*, so that would be critical. Gareth wasn't native to the planet, but even he had been impressed. The *Accord Ball* was the social event of the season, and everyone who was anyone on the planet had been trying to get tickets to attend.

It was a fundraiser, so the major players either

bought seats, or an entire table, for astronomical sums that supported the *Accord* Hall of Arts, the gravitational center of Grace culture. Lesser players were admitted as far as the front hall, where everyone could watch the beautiful people arrive, and then they were allowed into the hall itself after dinner, where they could mingle.

Rumor had it that the deals done every year at this event represented a serious percentage of the planetary output. At least in total cash.

How the Constabulary had gotten three tickets, Gareth didn't know, but obviously, strings had been pulled. Or they had the cash for something like this in their operating budget.

Or they just sent a few officers undercover every year on general principle.

He checked the time on his nightstand and decided he was close enough to ready. A quick look in the mirror hung on the wall to confirm everything, and he stuffed his new pocketcomm into the breast pocket of his blazer. The palm-sized stun pistol was on his thigh, hidden away inside the pant leg. He picked his beret up off the nightstand and went to the door.

He was supposed to wear the beret inside, but that just didn't fit with how he was raised, so it could wait until he was in the auto-car.

Grodray and Baker were down in the Operations Center when he arrived, chatting with Talyarkinash. Interestingly, while he was in the so-called grinder outfit, undercover, both of them where in their uniforms. Baker had even gone so far as to wear her outer tunic, like she was taking this sort of thing quite seriously.

Both women turned to him when he entered and gave him a critical once-over. Actually, all seven women in sight did the same, but Gareth tried to ignore that fact. And the intense interest and smiles on those faces.

"Beret?" Talyarkinash asked, so Gareth put it on, draping it just right.

"Yes," she said a moment later. "You'll do. Quite nicely."

Gareth blushed at her tone. It was not entirely friendly. Or it was, but not just that. No, he was the center of a lot of attentions, right now, like a beautiful woman who had walked into a room full of sailors who had been to space for too long.

Uncomfortable. Unpleasant turnabout. He would have made a note to say something about that sort of behavior when he got home, but he quashed that thought before it ever took shape.

There was no home. Not anymore. There was the *Accord of Souls*. And whatever he did to fit in here. For the rest of his life.

Gareth found himself standing at attention, like this was an inspection, so he forced himself to relax. It was an inspection, and he had apparently passed, from the looks, but he wasn't being graded.

Much.

"We'll depart first," Grodray announced simply, coming over to stand close.

He was a tall man, but skinny. Standing next to Gareth just emphasized his own, massive bulk.

Gareth nodded.

"You just smile and make small talk, Gareth," he said with a friendly grin. "Nobody knows you here except us, so it makes a good way to quietly introduce you to *Accord* society in a way that doesn't require a lot of legend-building on your part. You be aloof and mysterious. Talk art as if you'll be writing all this up for some magazine under a pseudonym later, and everyone will be polite."

"Then what?" he asked, still a little fuzzy on the overall picture.

"Then we'll see who nibbles at the bait," Baker said. "Nobody knows who you are, so you can make a whole range of new connections that can turn into contacts later."

"Okay," Gareth agreed. "I get that, but why don't I have business cards to hand out when they ask? I'm really just supposed to give them my first name and a comm box?"

"It forces them to perk up," Grodray said. "Makes you a galactic man of mystery, especially as an unknown who could afford a seat at this table, and had the connections to get in. Everyone will want to know who you are. Make them work at it."

"Okay," he shrugged. "Never really done undercover work, but I can at least talk art."

"And on *Orgoth Vortai*, that is all that matters, Gareth," Talyarkinash smiled up at him, reaching out a hand to flatten his lapel a little and run her hand down the wool of his blazer. Maybe a little too long. "I can't wait for you to tell me all the details later."

"And that's our cue," Grodray said. "Your vehicle

will arrive in ten minutes, so you should arrive just as the red carpet starts to get interesting. Remember, aloof and mysterious."

Gareth nodded and watched them head to the door. He had his pocketcomm, his wallet, and his stunner. If he was lucky, he wouldn't embarrass himself, or the nice man who had walked him so carefully through so much art history.

All he had now was that and those four books of modern art history and biography he had largely memorized.

Hopefully, it would be enough.

THE RED CARPET

IN ONE OF the books the older gentleman had suggested Gareth read, walking the red carpet was occasionally referred to as "The Pole Dance," which conjured up images of a scantily-clad woman doing all manner of athletic maneuvers on and with a floor-to-ceiling brass pole on a stage. Similar to burlesque, but far more physical in nature and requiring a great deal more effort to make look effortless.

And a little seedy, when you got right down to it. Tonight's arrival, too.

The auto-taxi deposited him at the curb behind a massive, hopefully-only-gold-*plated* limousine that delivered a well-dressed Grace and his barely-covered companion. They walked up the red carpet and were politely accosted at each of several reporter station, with cameras rolling. Famous people. Gareth hadn't seen either face to be sure, but he had narrowed the options down to about four, all of them important.

He himself emerged to a flash of lights and

whistles, but the man holding the vehicle's door made it clear that he was to simply amble inside, in full view of everyone, but not stop and chat with any of the reporters, unless specifically accosted.

Aloof and mysterious.

And really, freaking self-conscious, but he mustered himself under the gravity of the scene and strode forward in a relaxed manner. He could ignore the various whistles and cat-calls emerging from the dimly-lit crowd behind the barriers and holding up cameras.

Right?

Five reporters, each interviewing someone. Gareth breezed by them at a slow cadence, glancing right and left, but not seeing anything outside his imagination.

Four identical Nari men, dressed almost as silly as the Pope's Swiss Guard, defended the main hall from the riff-raff. The looks of appraisal sent his way were more along the lines of checking out the guy that had just walked into the wrong bar, to see if anybody really felt like doing anything about it. He had a head and at least one hundred pounds on the any of them, so they smiled.

"Ticket, please?" the closest one asked as Gareth approached.

He pulled the ornate card from an inner pocket and handed it over.

"Gareth?" the man asked in obvious confusion. "No last name?"

"That's right," he smiled ambiguously.

Let people fill in their own stories, Baker and Grodray and others had told him, time and again.

That was the key to undercover work. Keep it all vague and you don't have to track your lies later.

"Very good, sir," the Nari handed the card back and stepped to one side.

And with that, Gareth was in the Great Hall itself.

Because of the Chaa, and their lasting impact on the culture, everything was huge. The building was an eclectic mix of Ionic and Gothic that shouldn't have worked, but did. White marble flecked and striped with precious metals held up the roof and covered the floor.

The ceiling in here was forty meters at the peak of the low-pitched roof, with colorful banners hanging from everywhere and idly drifting in the breezes generated by open doors and the air conditioning system. The red carpet continued a four-meter-wide path up a flight of twenty, deep stairs. A Vanir could walk them individually, but anyone shorter would take two steps on each.

At the top of the stairs was an impressive bronze bust, fifteen feet tall, of a cyclopean Grace, tentacles in wild disarray and one, angry eyeball scowling out of the middle of his forehead.

Gareth checked the small placard at the bottom as he approached. He had seen pictures of the enormous head, but had never realized how big *"The Art Critic"* was in real life. Or what a lovely play on words it was, subtly tweaking all the artists in here and their fiercest enemies.

It put a smile on his face as he entered the atrium of the space at the top of the stairs, trying not to ogle the people around him. There were seventeen species represented in the *Accord of Souls*, and all of them appeared to be present tonight, in an array of outfits that left him too stunned to even comprehend, let alone describe.

Except there was a lot of skin visible, on both male and female, as well as fur, scales, and bark, depending on the direction he turned. Gareth concentrated on keeping his mouth from falling open, and headed in the direction of the open bar on the side wall.

He wasn't there to be noticed, unlike many of the people around him. If pressed, he could only name on sight perhaps two dozen, at best, of the three hundred or so that would be joining him for dinner. Many would be offended at his ignorance, however unintentional, so he would keep to himself.

The bartender was a tall, skinny, Grace woman. Lanky and over six feet tall, she was probably used to looking down on her patrons. The expression on her face as she turned to her right to serve him was sour.

She stared at the center of his chest for a moment, and then leaned back to see him smiling above her. Her own smile seemed to emerge from behind the dour shell.

"Sir?" she asked, voice turning hopeful, after the gruffness she had sent after the previous victim.

"Red wine," Gareth said simply. "The house blend is good enough for now."

Gareth had no way of guessing which of the dozen bottles in front of him he might like, and wasn't going to more than sip this glass anyway.

She overpoured him anyway and handed the glass up. Gareth took it with a nod.

"Thank you, ma'am," he said, turning away before she pursued any conversation.

He did not understand the effect he had on women, but there was no denying it. Gareth knew he was considered attractive, but had never seemed all that impressive, back home.

Or maybe he just never paid any attention? There was only one woman for him, even if he might never see her again.

Gareth took a sip and meandered into the slowly-thickening crowd.

"NO, IT'S JUST HIDEOUS," Gareth overheard two Grace, and older man and slightly-younger woman, well-dressed if conservative, discussing a painting that was hanging on a pillar.

Back home, art was something you observed from a safe distance, frequently behind a velvet rope, with the picture itself perhaps protected by a sealed, transparent container against aging.

But this was *Orgoth Vortai*, and these were the Grace. That was far too pedestrian.

One approached the painting and leaned close enough that a dozen or more head tentacles could touch the picture, absorbing a full-sensory experience of smell, taste, and texture to go along with the light. Many other installations in here included a musical element as well, so all senses would be engaged.

To allow the pitifully-under-sensed (the Grace's occasional term for the rest of the *Accord*), there was a small table to one side, near the picture. Sets-of-three shot glasses held a red, an umber, and a green liquid: just a taste of each, with a number indicating the order to consume them.

Gareth stepped to one side of the two Grace, still arguing, and studied the painting itself. The oil appeared to be a land- and sky-scape at sunset, perhaps. Fierce crimsons bled up into salmony-orange and down into violets, but the over-all image was scarlet in nature.

Gareth nodded to himself and emptied a red glass into his mouth first. It held barely enough to give him a taste, but that was the point. Umber followed quickly, and then green.

One held the three in one's mouth for a moment, swishing them around like a *sommelier* at a good wine, before swallowing. It was a complicated taste, almost sour at the outset fading down to an earthy sweetness after a few seconds.

"Mm-hmm," Gareth hummed to himself.

The nearer Grace turned to him.

"Utterly atrocious, am I correct?" he almost demanded.

Gareth checked the image of the artist herself by leaning well forward, just to make sure, before he leaned back and turned to the two critics. They didn't appear to be man and wife, although they might be of a similar age.

And he had absolutely no idea if the picture was any good. Or bad. Or how a Grace might experience it differently from a Vanir, or an Elohynn, like the one he saw over there.

But it didn't matter, as the old master had explained to him this morning. Art was art.

Gareth fell back on the best line the man had taught him, for exactly situations like this.

"I like the way she exhausts her reds," he opined breezily. "Refreshing."

Both gawked, and then leaned close to taste it again, afraid they had missed something terribly important that a Vanir, no less, had caught.

Gareth giggled privately to himself and departed before he was called on to explain the random remark. As if he could.

Art was art.

He made his way to the next installation, wondering what any of it meant.

"SERIOUSLY?" Morty demanded. "The *Accord Ball*? That bastard wants us to hang around outside like paparazzi for him, and he'll mingle with us after dinner? Screw that shit."

Xiomber shrugged. He handed the letter over to Morty and took a step back. Likely moving out of range before he got an angry fist to the snout.

Morty controlled his temper and read the note. Yes, that was exactly what it said. He and his egg-brother had tickets to the after party, while Omerlon would be at the banquet itself, being seen and famous.

"Hey," Xiomber said to get his attention. "There's another card in here. It's for a tailor who owes the man a favor. We're supposed to call him and get fitted for something nice, on Omerlon's dime."

Morty found that at least mollifying. Power, showing itself off. Omerlon was one of the power players on this planet. He was making that point, aggravating as it was.

But it he was willing to throw in a new suit as an enticement, Morty was willing to be enticed. He had worn nothing but grungy jeans and T-shirts for so long he might not even own anything nice enough for a public event like this. So even if they didn't end up getting a job offer they liked, they'd come out ahead.

Not that he'd be able to wear it in prison, but at that point, maybe something else would come up.

"Fine," Morty groused. "Anybody we know?"

"Nope," Xiomber said helpfully. "Want me to look him up?"

"Yes, please," he said. "Don't want to end up looking like a clown here."

"More like a clown?" Xiomber asked serenely.

Morty growled at the Yuudixtl. Xiomber laughed and pulled out a pad, typing furiously with one hand.

"Let's see," Xiomber said after a few moments. "Shit's gone really weird, this season, with an emphasis on flesh and glitter, if I read the guy's brochure correctly."

"We're scientists," Morty reminded his egg-brother. "We're supposed to look like nerds. Dark and severe would be my preference."

"Yeah, you ain't got the gams to pull off an outfit like this," Xiomber turned the screen to show him something a self-respecting Nari woman might hesitate to wear to the beach, let alone a ball. "We doing this?"

"Make the call and set us up an appointment," Morty groused some more. "I'll find us a place close for dinner reservations. Might as well try and make this stupid charade work."

Seriously? They wanted a quiet, sit-down kind of meeting to talk turkey with Omerlon, and the man wanted a spectacle.

Were all the criminals these days turning into congenital idiots?

DINNER

"GARETH?" the Borren woman seated on his left asked as she turned away from a conversation on her other side. "That's it? No last name."

"More mysterious that way," he offered, turning away from the overweight, middle-aged Vanir guy on his right that had wanted to talk about investing in art futures.

Whatever that was.

"I see," the woman leaned a little closer.

Borren were even taller than Vanir, so it made sense that they would be seated at the same table, itself a foot taller than normal. And Gareth had only seen a few of her type, and only at a distance, and not actually talked to one, so he couldn't tell her age at a glance.

She wore a headpiece in turquoise that sat on her bald skull like an ancient Chinese temple, as much as he could find words to compare it, looking at her. The species was apparently hairless, with spots bigger than freckles on their pate, as well as interesting color patterns like a giraffe trailing down all the parts of her shoulders, chest, and stomach that were naked flesh.

Which was most of them.

Twin ridges of bone emerged from the sides of the large, flat nose and flared away over the eyes, providing shadows that looked rather like eyebrows. Her eyes were simply huge, at least twice the size of Gareth's, with the points at the inner bottom and outer top corners of an invisible square.

She wore a dress that seemed to cover her back and encase the long, giraffe-like neck, covering only the tops of her shoulders and her arms down to the wrists. White, flexible, plastic sheets had been wrapped around her thorax like an open-fronted corset, resting on her hip bones and coming up to more or less cover her breasts from the sides.

More or less.

The fleshy top of her belly button was pierced, with a ruby pendant dangling in the hole. And if he was understanding the physics involved, he had to guess that her nipples were pierced as well, connected by a silver or platinum chain, hidden by the open-front corset device, connecting them. Not a question that he sought to answer, thank you kindly.

Gareth cleared his throat, sipped his wine, and concentrated on her face. It was weird, but looking up kept him from looking down. The way she leaned towards him and seemed to flex her long torso didn't help his state of mind.

"And what do you do, Gareth-with-no-name?" she purred warmly.

Gareth fell back as hard as he could on the training and books. Those had been for this question, but the role-play he had done to get ready had been with fully-clothed agents, many of them men.

This was…

"I'm a writer," he offered, as blandly as he could. "Mostly magazine work."

"Anything I'd know?" her gravity seemed to be off, or her balance. She kept easing closer, like a tide coming in.

"All written under a pen name," he tried to relax. "Fewer enemies that way."

"You must have friends, to get this invitation," she smiled easily with soft, blue lips.

"Favors for important people," Gareth suggested. "And I'll write this all up tomorrow."

"And when will it be in print?" she was almost breathing on him now. It was like dating that volleyball player in junior high school, when she had been almost a head taller than him, too.

"Who's to say," Gareth shrugged, using that as an opportunity to eke out a little more distance.

If he wasn't careful, she'd be in his lap very shortly.

Not what Constable Baker had planned for him tonight.

Hopefully.

The steward rescued him, delivering a mixed salad and refreshing the bread bowl. Another one filled water and took drink orders.

Gareth had no idea what the salad was. And didn't really care. The colors were probably fake anyway, or they grew pink carrots here. Didn't matter. He used the fork in one hand and a hunk of bread in the other to defend his turf like the Russians at Moscow facing the invaders. Any of them.

The woman seemed more bemused than insulted. The man on Gareth's other side was still bending the ear of the man on his far side about investment opportunities and tax breaks.

All conversation seemed, of universal volition, to subside for an hour, replaced by the tinkling of knives and folks on plates and glasses being set down loud enough to clunk. Salad was followed by a cold soup that would have been proudly served by any Ukrainian café in the solar system.

Gareth hadn't ordered the main course. Apparently, that had been handled by whoever got him the invitation. They had selected the beef. He hoped it was beef. Now was not the time to ask. Nor was this the place. The sauce was lavender. And rather sweet/sour in the way of certain Chinese dishes he had encountered in his travels.

Gareth pretended he had a boneless ribeye in a redwine reduction, and attacked it with gusto. And it was close enough, with the occasional sip of red wine and some buttered bread in between bites.

When the stewards removed his plate and filled his coffee cup, Gareth found the woman on his left suddenly much closer than he remembered her chair being before.

"Diệu Ahn," she introduced herself. "Since we don't have last names tonight."

Gareth shivered, but only inside, he hoped. That

sounded like too much of an invitation on her part. Letting her hair down, although she didn't have any, just exquisite, tiny ears and that huge headpiece.

Gareth lifted the coffee cup like it was a shield, holding his left elbow out in such a way as to hopefully keep her at arm's length. But then the other patrons began to rise and make their way towards the front of the building, from the auditorium at the back where dinner had been served.

Before he was fully standing, Diệu Ahn had her arm wrapped around his.

"I think you're one of those fashion writers that always goes by a secret identity at these sorts of things," she murmured down to him. "That or a secret agent. What do you think, Gareth?"

"Something like that," he replied evenly. It was even true, more or less.

Just not the parts she was expecting.

"Have you seen the entire hall?" she continued, leading him towards a grand flight of stairs he had ignored earlier, when he had been scouting the people more than the terrain.

These steps were more polished white marble, overlaid with a burgundy carpet that bullnosed at each step.

"I have not," he replied.

Gareth felt like a dog on a leash, or one with his head out the window, as she politely led him up the stairs. That she was at least seven inches taller or more, depending on the heels below that dress, didn't help. Everything about her was turquoise and white tonight, except her skin, which was too pink to be alabaster, and those freckles, which might cover her entire body in geometric shapes.

Gareth really, REALLY didn't want to do any math tonight.

The mezzanine was lovely. Gareth regretted not coming up here earlier. The view was perfect to observe all the beautiful people below, while keeping them at a polite and impersonal distance. He and Diệu Ahn shared the balcony with a number of other folks, some he recognized from dinner, and a large number of photographers making their living. Steward with trays came by, and she snagged them both glasses of what Gareth guessed were champagne, from the color and bubbles.

She giggled as they tickled her nose. It was a pretty, girlish, distracting sound that kept Gareth's attention wandering to places it had no business going.

Pippa. Only Pippa.

At the far end of the hall, the flood gates had apparently been breached. A wave of species poured into the grand hall from the front, those people with second-class tickets to the after-party.

Dinner had been showy and self-congratulatory, as various awards had been given out while everyone chowed down. Now came the grand event. Everyone coming in with the tides had a camera in one hand. Drones were forbidden indoors tonight, and nobody wanted to miss anything.

Diệu Ahn still had her free hand around his elbow. Gareth watched her set her glass down on the wide, marble balustrade and reach inside her corset, thankfully below her breast instead of across it. She did something and withdrew her hand, reaching towards him.

Gareth nearly flinched. He wasn't sure what to expect, but his mind kept seeing a giant spider in her hand. His nerves were apparently shot.

Instead, she had pulled a business card from in pocket inside the corset-thingee. Rather like his blazer had pockets inside, but his were empty.

She leaned in close and languidly slid her hand inside his blazer, searching for his pocket for several seconds in the wrong places with a smile and a quiet, coquettish giggle. Finally, she dropped the card and withdrew her hand. Gareth's breath was short.

"Got something for me?" she purred, twisting her torso around a little to make it obvious where he might put such a thing.

Inwardly, he said a small prayer of thanks to Constable Baker. Even accidentally.

"My, uh, boss actually forbid me from carrying any tonight," Gareth replied dejectedly, at least he hoped it sounded that way. "Under threat of extreme sanction. And she was serious."

"She?" Diệu Ahn looked interested in a potential rival to battle.

"Complete and total hardass editor," Gareth freelanced the relationship. It sounded close enough, from what he had seen of newspapers on the video tube. "If I wasn't bound under a tight contract, I'd shop my services elsewhere."

Wrong thing to say. Her eyes perked right up.

"Oh," Diệu Ahn smiled. "Need a good lawyer to help you break a contract? I have several on staff."

Gareth blinked and remembered his manners.

"It dawns on me that we've only talked about my life tonight," he tried to deflect the statuesque woman. "What do you do, Diệu Ahn?"

She grabbed her glass and sipped, telegraphing a shrug with her entire body in such a way that Gareth kept losing focus on her eyes.

"I'm an art patron," she said modestly. "I buy, I sell. I collect things that catch my eye."

That last in a purr that felt like a bear-trap closing.

"I'll have to remember to call you next week for an interview," Gareth suggested.

"Call?" Diệu Ahn smiled. "That, too. Nudge, perhaps?"

Gareth smiled and sipped his wine, hoping that he wasn't beet red right now.

Pippa.

She seemed to sense some of his discomfort and withdrew her fangs, just a little. She tugged at his arm, turning him to the right, where he could see a new gallery through a narrow archway.

"We should enjoy the art," Diệu Ahn announced in a quiet, authoritative voice. "Broaden our horizons."

Gareth nodded and read the name of the space over the door. His heart really wanted to stop beating right now. Just keel over and die, but it refused.

Inter-Species Erotica it read in a lovely, Helvetica font. Small enough to be discrete.

In a Grace museum. The sort of place where art exhibits were expected to be *interactive*.

Gareth's eyes refused to dwell on it. He was undercover, making contacts which he hoped would lead him to useful places in the underworld. Baker and Grodray had them. His job was start building his own network.

However unsavory that task might turn out to be.

Instead, his focus drifted back to the crowd below. The mad rush was over and people were settling into clusters and currents.

Gareth stopped dead, dragging Diệu Ahn to a halt as well.

"Hey," he muttered absently.

"What is it, Gareth?" she asked, leaning close and rubbing herself against his side.

"I know those guys," he said aloud.

Down in the main hall. Morty looked up and locked eyes with him. The Yuudixtl said something that was covered by the noise in the auditorium, but that was okay. Gareth was pretty sure it would have gotten the lizardman's mouth washed out with soap, were either of their mothers here right now.

Morty turned and nudged Xiomber, the two them talking to a fat Elohynn with a couple of obvious bodyguards.

The frozen tableau held for a moment, and then the two Yuudixtl bolted.

THE CHASE

"HEY, YOU TWO," Gareth yelled, but Morty and Xiomber weren't having any of it.

He was still tangled up with Diệu Ahn, so he took the moment to set the wine glass down and smile up at her.

"Fashion writer with a secretive past?" he said quickly. "Also secret agent. Those two are bad guys. My most profuse apologies, but I must give chase now,"

She leaned in and quickly kissed him on the lips before he could react.

"Call me," she said, stepping back and letting go of his arm.

Gareth threw caution to the wind and grabbed her to return the quick kiss, only the third woman he had ever done that to, and the second one taller than him.

He turned and spotted the two runners. They were making their way to the front door, with the fat Elohynn lumbering along in their wake. Given the nature of things, Gareth assumed another bad guy with a guilty conscience.

Considering what Morty and Xiomber did, he wondered if the man was another crime boss, like Marc. One way to find out.

The stairs were too flat and wide to take them more than two at a time, and there were people on them that were too fragile for him to brush against. Especially with a forty foot drop off the side.

He ran anyway, weaving like a wingback that had made it through the defensive line and was facing open field and a goal line. He had always been athletic and a jock. As a Vanir, he was even better than he had been then, moving like a ballerina.

At the bottom of the stairs, two of the fat person's bodyguards had decided to fight a rear-guard action of some sort. One was a Vanir like him. The other a burly Grace. Gareth smiled.

The *Accord of Souls* was a peaceful place, by design. Team sports were all about skill and athleticism, but they had nothing like rugby or American football.

Too violent.

Too bad.

Neither of the goons had a weapon in hand, so Gareth didn't bother trying to pull his stunner from his knee. Instead, he transformed on the fly into a halfback, punching a hole in the defensive line for his tailback to streak to glory. He lowered a shoulder and pulled in his right arm close to his body, just like the old days.

The Vanir facing him was awkwardly balanced

and had obviously never faced a blocker coming through the line. You had to get under the runner in order to stop him. Gareth had been a defensive end in school, faster and smaller than the monsters in the interior, and taller than the linebackers.

Now he was bigger and faster than any player he had ever faced. And running full tilt. He smashed into the Vanir and bounced the poor man onto his ass while stiff-arming the Grace to the face in a way that would have been good for a fifteen-yard penalty and a stern talking-to from Coach, if the man were around to witness it.

Needs must.

Both villains were down and Gareth was in the backfield, with the safeties still trailing their receivers and their backs to the play. He put on a burst of speed towards the front door and the goal line.

Out of the corner of his eye, he spied Baker and Grodray suddenly wake up to the situation, but he was moving as fast as his upgraded legs could carry him, and not even Eveth Baker could run him down now, as much as she might want to dispute that in other circumstances.

From the top of the entry stairwell, he saw the trio exit through the front door, the glass thrust open hard enough to ring when the metal frame slammed against another door. Neither broke, but that just meant they were reinforced.

And the Elohynn was in the lead now, with the two lizardmen trailing him as fast as those stubby legs could churn.

These steps were so wide that Gareth had to take

them individually so he didn't trip and face-plant going down. It slowed him some, but not enough. He could see a plain van land outside and the trio enter through the back. It wasn't an auto-car, so there was probably no way that the Constables behind him could override the controls. At best, they would have to call for backup pursuit, which may and may not arrive fast enough to corner them.

Gareth hit the closing door hard enough that it did shatter this time. Or at least spiderweb into a million pieces held in place by a film of clear plastic. The panel van was just taking off and he had only a split second to make a decision.

He jumped onto side of the vehicle by the driver's door as it leapt into the air, the ground falling away quickly behind him.

Now was when it would probably get ugly.

PAPARAZZI

MORTY HAD TO ADMIT IT. He looked good tonight. Purple tights tucked into low, pull-on boots in a black suede. Lavender tunic almost to his knees, with a white belt and lots of showy pockets embroidered in white.

Even if the night was a bust, he could get into the nicest restaurants and parties in this rig. That dude must have really owed Omerlon a big favor. Even Xiomber was presentable, though he looked more like a banker, or a mortician, in severe black pants and blazer over a black shirt and black tie. Seriously, that lizard was a hole in the night, standing next to a supernova of awesome.

It wasn't Omerlon's champagne, but the house stuff was still damned good, as the three of them chatted about nothing and sipped. Omerlon was wearing a white toga tonight that made him look like how the Chaa were always portrayed on television. Even down to the purple stripe around the edge.

"Enjoying yourselves, gentlemen?" Omerlon asked, looking like a cat with the best cream in town.

"Indeed," Xiomber replied with a nod. "Ravishing."

Morty expected his egg-brother to click his heels together or something. What had come over the boy?

"This is a mark of my control of *Orgoth Vortai*," Omerlon swept a hand out and nearly whacked a goon in the face.

Both bodyguards took a step back in unison, so Morty presumed that the man gestured a lot when he spoke. Useful to know.

"We're convinced," Xiomber said. "Right now, we're down to brass tacks. Retirement plans and profit sharing."

"Is that how Maximus did it?" Omerlon half-sneered and looked half-interested in the information.

"Among other things," Morty heard Xiomber reply.

Morty's attention was suddenly riveted onto a figure up on the balcony. Huge, even for a Vanir, if the Borren next to him was a good measure of size. The blond hair was long enough that it would get shaggy soon, and the beard was a pretty good disguise, but Morty had helped Talyarkinash with the basic upgrade designs.

That was Gareth. As a Vanir. Here. At this party.

Looking this way.

Their eyes met. Locked.

"*Fardel*," Morty ejaculated before he could contain it.

"What?" Xiomber turned towards him, but Morty

nudged him and gestured to the balcony with his chin.

Even Omerlon grew interested enough to glance over his shoulder.

"Oh, shit," Xiomber muttered under his breath before raising his voice just enough for Omerlon to hear. "We're blown."

Morty was gone as soon as Xiomber said the word. If Gareth was here, there would be others.

There. The crazy Vanir cop chick from *Hurquar*. The other guy was probably her partner, the two them in dress uniforms tonight while Gareth had been in mufti.

Definitely time to skedaddle.

He could hear Xiomber right behind him, those mortician shoes slapping angrily at the marble with every step, while Morty's boots squeaked.

A heavier tread close behind was Omerlon, trusting their instincts and joining them in flight.

Across the hall and past the giant head of the crazy Grace. Morty cursed whatever damned Grace architect had decided that stairs should slow you down to enjoy the art. Gareth was running after them with Vanir legs, and Morty couldn't just throw himself forward if he wanted to make it to the bottom without any broken limbs.

And that fat bastard Omerlon cheated. Hit the top of the steps and stuck his wings out sideways to glide to the ground floor while Morty and his egg-brother were only halfway down.

At least he opened the door for them, hard enough

that the catch hadn't swung it back in their faces by the time they got there.

Morty heard the crime boss calling for his car on a comm, so maybe they had a chance to get out of this, if they stayed close to the guy. He had been planning to hit the door and bolt sideways, making the cops pick who to chase down in the darkness, but a personal vehicle just might get away.

The truck landed. It looked like something a plumber might own, minus only the name and comm number on the side, but the back sprang open and the fat angel waddled up the steps inside.

Morty was right on his ass when he cleared the doorway, and Xiomber slammed it shut with all his might as he got in.

"Go." Morty yelled at the driver, a head visible through a window to the cab.

Omerlon had landed himself in a throne, gasping for air like a grounded whale shark. Morty grabbed Xiomber and pushed him into a pair of seats at the front, backs to the driver and facing the fat man as the engines surged with power.

He took the moment to hook his seatbelt, laughing to himself while Xiomber did the same. They had both picked that up from Gareth, the very man chasing them.

The driver had slammed the throttle to the stops. The whole vehicle seemed to squat for a moment on its haunches, before it leapt into the night sky like a jaguar pouncing on a bird in a tree.

Morty and Xiomber shared a secret grin as Omerlon was nearly dumped on his ass before he managed to grab onto the arms of his seat. The truck was pulling something like two G's, more or less straight up. Hopefully enough to get some distance before a local cop car could start after them.

After that, it was a matter of getting underground and hiding before the Constables brought in everybody in town down here to chase them.

A thump on the outside hull beside Morty sounded an awful lot like a big Vanir landing on the running boards next to the driver. A moment later, a thump that sounded like a fist hitting the window.

Knowing Omerlon, they were bullet-proof, but the crime boss had only been expecting a normal cop. That sort of thing might not stop Gareth, if Talyarkinash had actually pulled it off.

This was about to get ugly.

"Boss, we got a passenger on the outside," the driver yelled as the vehicle kept surging upwards into the night sky.

"Dump him off," Omerlon called back.

"Hang on," the driver replied.

Morty and Xiomber were already buckled in. Omerlon managed to do the same just in time as the vehicle turned almost fifty degrees to the left.

It was like being on a ride at a carnival.

Another thump on the side of the panel truck. Louder.

Angrier, if Morty had to put a better adjective to it.

Yeah, that sounded like a modified human losing his temper out there.

"Who is this guy?" Omerlon fixed them with a hard stare.

"Constable," Xiomber offered. "We've run into him a few times. Mean SOB. Even worse than Grodray and Baker."

"And he just happened to recognize you at the Ball?" Omerlon sneered.

Morty just shrugged. No way to explain that without getting himself killed.

Outside the vehicle pitched again. The thumps on the driver's window got louder.

Suddenly, the glass shattered, letting a ripping wind into the interior of the van.

The vehicle leveled off some, as the driver was suddenly too busy wresting with Gareth to try to shake him loose.

Omerlon reached inside his toga as the noise grew worse. He came out with a pistol and Morty felt all the blood pool in his stomach.

"Since you know the guy, I'll let you die with him," Omerlon snarled.

Before Morty could react, Omerlon shot the flight console twice. In a flash, the fat man moved to the rear door, pushed it open and stepped out into the night.

"See you in hell," trailed back into the cabin with the wind.

The words were quiet, but Morty could still hear them clearly. All the engines had gone silent as the craft slowed to a halt, paused, and began to free-fall.

RELENTLESS

GARETH FELT his upgraded muscles strain to hold onto the side of the truck as it pitched over until his back was parallel with the ground. He had a boarding rail in one hand, where the driver could reach up when climbing in, and a running board under his feet.

And about three thousand feet of warm night sky below him.

He managed to swing his right foot loose and get it under the running board, using that and the rail as a pair of anchor points to hold himself up.

Gareth punched the driver's window with an angry fist, but it bounced off. Safety glass, he presumed.

The truck righted itself for a moment, and then rolled again hard, like an angry gator with fresh prey.

Now he was losing his temper. They could manage to dump him, but Gareth wouldn't be killed, unlike any other officer in the service. That still made this attempted murder.

He snarled.

One thing Gareth had learned about his new form was the ability to trigger it in pieces, for lack of a better term. He didn't have to fully transform his body, but could instead just dramatically escalate his strength beyond anything an unmodified Vanir could do. It helped that rage just fueled him right now.

He leaned into a minor transformation, even as the vehicle righted itself a second time. Instead of just punching the glass, the Star Dragon put all his might into annihilating it.

Nothing was capable of resisting that might. And it did not.

Even the most bullet-proof glass wasn't dragon-proof,

Gareth reached in with a hand that had started to turn scaly and green. The driver grappled with him, trying to do something. Knock him loose, perhaps? Force his hands away from the controls?

Gareth would never know. A raygun suddenly blasted the entire console in front of the driver and the truck's engines died.

"See you in hell," a sour voice rang clear in the sudden silence, and then the vehicle's upward trajectory abruptly slowed as it discovered gravity.

Gareth snarled.

Now, attempted murder of a Constable had moved up to mass murder. At least four people, including himself, Morty, Xiomber, and the driver, plus whoever else might be in back, plus anyone who would be killed when an out-of-control panel van slammed into the ground at terminal velocity.

And there was nothing he could do about it.

Or was there?

Gareth was supposed to keep his powers secret. A surprise weapon to spring on the bad buys at the best time. At least, those that hadn't already been there, or heard the stories.

But if he did that, innocent people would die tonight. Even criminals who didn't deserve this end.

Gareth let go of everything but his left hand on the boarding rail and let the rest of the transformation take hold.

Even a Star Dragon couldn't lift a heavy vehicle like this, but he had to try.

"Mayday," the dragon's immensely deep voice called out, hoping that someone was monitoring the channel.

Someone who could help.

"Gareth, this is Baker," her voice came back instantly. "What's your situation?"

Gareth felt the truck reach the top of the parabola and pause for a second at its highest point. He shifted around so that he could grab the two front windows with his front paws and hammered his claws into the armored sides of the back. His wings caught the night air and bit as the immense dead weight pulled him towards the planet below.

"Total vehicle failure," Gareth said precisely. "One Elohynn criminal in flight. At least three others trapped in the vehicle. Can anyone help?"

The strain on his shoulders felt like they would tear loose at any moment. He flapped, but barely made any headway, until he had a thought.

Gareth pushed his entire body backwards, letting the weight of the vehicle shift itself forward. The nose of the truck went down, and Gareth could see better where he was going.

He didn't have to slam into the ground when it got here, but the others didn't have that option, and the ground would be here faster than anybody could arrive that might be able to prevent the giant anvil in his grip from smashing itself to pieces on the ground, plus any towers or restaurants that managed to be in the way of falling death.

"Can you make the river?" Baker asked calmly. "Ditch there where we might be able to rescue survivors?"

Might.

It was night, and that water would be dark and cold. The men inside would have seconds to escape, assuming the van survived impacting the water, before they were pulled to the dark, murky bottom.

And from this height, hitting water was going to be like hitting concrete, because there was no way he was going to flatten them out enough to matter in the next thirty seconds.

"Negative," he said.

Gareth looked other directions. The river was just too far away, and the towers beside it too tall. He'd probably end up slamming into one as he went by, trying to avoid killing people.

He was back to Ethics 101 at school. Do you choose to send the runaway vehicle crashing into a tree to save pedestrians, thereby killing the driver, or do nothing and let the vehicle kill the pedestrians instead?

How do you decide who has to die today?

In some ways, that wasn't even a thing to discuss. The three inside might have to die, but Gareth would not put anybody else at risk to die, possibly with them, rather than instead.

Blinking lights on the ground caught his eye. The tube station was close. But the entire facility was dark right now. Gareth had learned enough to know that meant there were no ferries currently in orbit overhead.

"Can you contact the station?" Gareth strained to make the words intelligible as he pushed everything he had into his shoulders, trying to turn the massive dead weight to starboard. At the very least, there were open fields in that direction, so he would only kill the two men who had brought him here, and the driver.

Hopefully.

"What station?" Baker asked.

"The tube station," Gareth roared. "Have them turn on the generators and open me a tube into space. Do it now."

He took a breath and leaned over to the left.

"Morty, can you hear me?" he called.

"Is that you, kid?" the Yuudixtl physicist called back in a hopeful voice.

"It is," Gareth replied. "Can you find the emergency oxygen masks?"

Every flying vehicle had to have them, by law, on the presumption that they might go through a wormhole at some point, and all of those were in space. Because the law said emergencies and mistakes happen, you had to be able to survive suddenly losing a vehicle seal and facing vacuum.

This vehicle was turning. Falling in a different direction, perhaps. Not into the heart of the art district, nor the Hall of Arts.

If he could only make it that far before his friends had to die.

"Got 'em, Gareth," Xiomber's voice came back. "What are you doing?"

"Put them on now," Gareth roared in a voice that much of the city below might have heard.

Baker had gone silent on him. Hopefully that meant that she was calling someone over at the tube station, waking them up. Doing something that would prevent a lot of unnecessary deaths tonight.

Gareth strained through the pain. It felt like his wings were being pulled out of their sockets to the point that he might not be able to escape when this thing hit the ground. He would just have to deal with that.

Or watch his friends die. He could always just let go right now and survive with nothing more than bruises and pulled muscles. Three presumed criminals would suffer the ultimate sanction, and they would never again be a threat to the *Accord of Souls*.

That wasn't why he had joined Earth Force. Wasn't what made him an agent of Sky Patrol.

Gareth St. John Dankworth was not a man who surrendered.

He pulled harder. Growled. Metal actually began

to deform under his grip as his claws ripped into the steel of the truck's carcass.

Ten seconds to impact.

Gareth howled in pain and frustration. They hadn't dreamed big enough, back when they created a Star Dragon. He should have gone for something big enough to lift a tank or a star shuttle off the ground.

Then Morty and Xiomber and the poor driver wouldn't be about to die from his failures.

Five seconds.

Light.

NIGHTFALL

THERE IS no air in space, Gareth thought to himself as the flash of light ended, replaced by an endless darkness broken by a billion points of light. He was suddenly in freefall and vacuum.

Beneath him, the air in the panel van exploded outwards through the shattered window and the opened back door, a snow storm that ended as abruptly as it had begun.

A pinging began in his right ear in spite of the soundlessness of space. It matched a flashing red light that suddenly reflected off his hide and tail.

Emergency beacon on the truck. Automatic. The vehicle has suffered a failure in space and the onboard systems had triggered their own mayday. His earpiece was picking up the distress beacon, and it was tucked in deep enough that he could feel it click in his bones.

Gareth's inner eyelids clicked shut and held in moisture, as did his nostrils. He kept his mouth shut and let his own unconscious systems come into play. Talyarkinash had designed the Star Dragon to survive in deep space. He was airtight and insulated against cold, air loss, and radiation for several hours, if his held breath lasted that long.

The men inside the van didn't have that option. If they were wearing their air masks, they could at least breathe, but vacuum damage and cold would do them in quickly. He needed to do something.

He hadn't come this far just to lose them now.

Without gravity's greedy clutches, he could move the panel truck more easily. It was a giant medicine ball in his hands now, rather than a Sisyphean impossibility. He flapped his wings and imagined bringing the vehicle to a stop, since he had nothing in the vicinity against which to measure his speed.

Still, it seemed to work. He let go with rear claws and right hand, and flowed himself around to the open front window. The one he had shattered earlier.

The driver was gone.

For a moment, Gareth panicked, looking every direction in case the man had been blasted into deep space by the sudden decompression, but he was alone in the darkness and silence.

Nothing.

He stuck his head into the window and looked at the rear. Morty and Xiomber, at least, had been back there, and hadn't gone out the back door either.

Then he saw why.

Inside the rear cabin was a giant bubble. One Grace and two Yuudixtl sat inside, pale white and darkest green, respectively.

Morty waved cheerfully. The driver flinched.

Huh. Emergency lifeboat system. He hadn't thought about that. Trigger it to inflate and then seal it up around you. Probably up to an hour of air, depending on how many people it had to contain.

"Gareth, this is Baker, can you hear me?" a tinny voice came in his ear.

"I can," he said.

It was weird, talking without moving his jaw. The bones in his head would carry the sound via induction to the microphone in his ear, with some distortion. No complicated speeches, but basic communication would work.

"Thank you," he continued. "It worked."

"What is your status?" she asked, obviously relieved.

"Vehicle dead in high orbit," Gareth murmured. "Three people in a survival bubble."

"Okay, stand by," she said. "We're trying to find a truck big enough to rescue you at the same time we do your prisoners. Nothing like that here."

Gareth considered his options. He actually couldn't remember seeing anything but a transport shuttle capable of holding his twenty-seven-meter-long dragon form, and he couldn't shift back to his base form without a space suit. Up here, there would be no time to get into one.

He'd be facing the same freezing death he had feared these three men had gotten into.

Then a thought struck him.

"Do you have an auto-car that had can open to space?" he asked.

There was a long pause before her voice returned.

"We do, but what about you?" she asked.

"Rescue them first," he said. "I have an idea for me."

"Okay," Baker said. "Stand by."

Gareth pulled his head back out the window and stuck a paw in instead, giving them a thumbs-up signal he hoped was universal. His current face wasn't capable of smiling like a Vanir or a Grace could, and he didn't have time to teach them.

Instead, he moved around the truck, finding the spots where his rear claws had actually managed to punch holes in the sides in spite of the armor.

Of course, in the *Accord of Souls*, everything was a beam weapon of some sort, rather than a high-velocity shell, so you needed insulation and thermal barriers, rather than inches of hardened steel plate and ceramics to protect you.

The men inside were trapped by the narrowness of the door. Gareth had no idea how much squeezing and reshaping the bubble could take, trying to pry it out of the back of the vehicle, and it would only take one mistake to kill the three men inside it.

He braced his feet into those holes again, but facing rearwards this time. In space, there is no gravity to hold you down. And no friction to stop you from moving, You are actually in constant freefall, but moving sideways such that it looks like you can never hit ground.

Everything becomes leverage.

Fortunately, Agents of Earth Force Sky Patrol had to be experts in extra-vehicular activities in order to earn their badge. Gareth had lost track of all the times he had needed to move outside a vehicle in deep space, from rescuing a lost puppy to stopping a runaway ship from destroying Shadow Base One, back in the Earth–Moon L2 LaGrange Point.

His dragon form was long enough to clamp onto the top of the truck and hold himself firmly, while also stretching his front to the aft of the craft. The door opened out and was just getting in the way, so that needed to go first.

Or did it?

He relaxed his chest and inspected the metal of the craft more closely. In this form, he could have licked it and gotten almost as good an understanding as a mass spectrometer, but that would waste precious air. Plus he might end up sticking his tongue to a frozen sign post.

He twisted around until he was looking in the rear. Morty and the others had turned to face him from much closer. Apparently, one of them had said something to the driver, because the Grace seemed a little more relaxed than before.

Like maybe he wasn't expecting a Star Dragon to have him for lunch.

Heh.

Gareth held up a single finger, again hoping it was a universal signal, and pushed the door closed until he felt it latch through his claws.

In space, nobody can hear you laugh. That was good, because this was the single silliest thing he had done since he came to the *Accord of Souls* seven weeks ago.

He let go.

It stayed where it was.

He flapped lazily until he was lined up with the passenger bottom corner of the truck.

There is no air in space, but he didn't actually use mechanical lift to do this, according to Talyarkinash Liamssen. It was all in his mind, somehow, a leftover from somewhere, or perhaps a trace of the very godhead that the Chaa had tapped when they moved past physical forms.

Was that why they had uplifted all the other species in the galaxy and left humans alone? Did we have the potential to someday join them on their exotic quest to find God and sit at his feet?

Gareth had always been punctual about Sunday school as a child. And visited Pastor Jacob whenever he had home leave, plus whichever priest was assigned to the base he was at. The religions really didn't matter that much to Gareth, as long as they *believed*. As ship's commander, he had even had to act as priest for his own crews, making special readings every seventh day to help bind them into a greater whole that was Earth Force Sky Patrol.

Gareth blinked in shock. He wondered if this radical idea was something he could ever share with anyone. The *Accord of Souls* was comprised of species that had been Uplifted by the Chaa and then set into their current form.

Did that mean that nobody but a human had that potential? Did it mean Marc Sarzynski really could achieve godhead if he worked at it hard enough? That Gareth could himself?

Whoa.

Still, not a problem for today. Right now, he needed to save these three men from certain death, and that meant that he needed to get them out of the vehicle safely.

The hatch was closed and latched. He hadn't seen it move. Everything *should* be safe enough.

Just to be sure, he started low and away, like a good curveball coming in over the plate.

The Star Dragon had a binary chemical weapon. It didn't need oxygen, as one of the two chemicals in the mix contained enough. More would help, but he needed controlled destruction today, and not psychological terror.

Gareth opened his mouth just a little. It was almost like that disgusting habit of chewing tobacco and spitting the juice into a cup. He had set down strict rules on any crew he commanded that something like that was not allowed aboard ship, because it could be so messy.

Squeezed his chest slowly and carefully. Aimed his snout and focused the sudden blast of superheated fluid.

And discovered that Newton was right, when he was suddenly tumbling backwards ass over teakettle.

He hadn't been pushing forward, and had done the equivalent of lighting a rocket engine in his mouth. Hopefully, nobody had a camera pointed this direction.

He flapped a few times and stopped his tumble, just the slightest bit queasy.

Getting closer, the tail of the truck was certainly

scorched, but not in a single spot, as he had planned. It looked more like a badly done crème Brule.

Okay, focus on incoming pressure and hold yourself stable this time, dummy.

He moved again to the right spot and focused his will. Another jet of flames.

This time, he flapped his wings, leaning into the heavy wind that was his own personal rocket engine in deep space. He'd need to remember this trick, sometime.

The blowtorch hit the corner of the truck and started it tumbling as well. Slower, but noticeable.

Crap.

Gareth quickly pounced on the vehicle and pulled that damned medicine ball until it felt like it was sitting in space again. The riders probably wouldn't notice a moderate spin, but he didn't need them puking on the inside of that emergency bubble and then having to sit in it for an hour or more.

Okay, fine.

Gareth stuck his toes back into the holes he had gouged earlier. Newton was right, and physics were physics. He would just have to do this upside down.

Third try.

He had a better idea of how to flame in space by now. And could bring it down to a fine, cutting blade of plasma. He was pretty sure the door was insulated, and probably a good chunk of the rear and sides, but the welds where the vehicle had been assembled would still be vulnerable.

It was just going to take patience.

Fine.

Up the sides, and he could see the welds weaken. He didn't want to actually penetrate the interior, because his breath weapon was too dangerous to the soft tissue of the emergency bubble.

No, this was just to soften them up a little.

"What are you doing?" Baker's voice came across the radio.

It sounded like she was watching him.

Gareth stopped flaming and looked up. Sure enough, an auto-car hung in space about thirty meters away. Almost close enough that he could touch both at the same time if he stretched, but far enough distant to stay out of his way.

The aft airlock hatch was open and she was standing in it, wearing a light EVA suit and clamped to the interior with a secondary line. Good professionalism on her part.

He wondered who was driving, if anyone, and what they though to see a dragon in space.

"Watch," Gareth smiled.

He returned to his work. Across the top. Down the driver's side. Back across the bottom.

"Could you move up and to my starboard?" Gareth asked.

"Stand by," she said.

Silence, so she was probably on a different channel, talking to the car or the driver.

Gareth puffed a few places that looked a little stronger than the rest, and then delicately opened the door. He leaned his head in and scanned as much as he could with his peripheral vision.

So far, so good. Probably would have set things on

fire if they were down on the surface, but there was no air to burn up here.

Morty and Xiomber looked quite thrilled at the spectacle. The Grace had turned almost green by now. Probably not the day he envisioned when he got out of bed.

Baker's car had moved off and out of the way. Physics was physics, and this was probably going to be impressive as hell when she replayed the video later for Grodray and whoever else was cleared for this level of secrecy.

Okay, now to get crazy.

Strength, like flight, was a matter of mind. Or mind over matter. Or something. He hadn't been strong enough to lift this truck when it was falling, but maybe Talyarkinash could upgrade him again later. Maybe a Greater Star Dragon form to improve upon the first?

But he didn't need to carry the damnable thing, just damage it.

Eight, razor-sharp, front claws found the weakened seams where the pieces had been welded together, once upon a time. But heat/cool cycles unquenched metal, had it ever been done right, and made things brittle.

And Gareth was still a little angry at having failed earlier. He sank the tips through the welds like butter and pulled.

In space, everything is relative leverage.

And dragonrage.

He heaved.

A seam parted. Not much, but a crack suddenly

ran nearly a meter. Good enough. He shifted his grip to the other side of the stern and did the same thing. This was easier. He had a feel for where it was going to tear.

The sides were going to be harder, except that he could just shift himself around the truck ninety degrees.

Oh, yeah.

He slithered to his right and found a new spot to dig in his toes. Couple of good, solid kicks and he was firmly anchored to the carcass.

This might even work.

Reach around the aft end and grab the side. This weld felt softer than the others. He wondered if the verticals hadn't been anchored as heavily as the horizontals. That would certainly make this easier.

Torque, and he could see a gap run the entire side of the vehicle.

Gareth had planned to hit the top next, but a lazy welding crew might make this far easier than he had planned. He shifted one hundred and eighty degrees this time, so he could get a grip on the passenger side and attack across.

Sure enough, this set of welds had been seals, rather than structural, like the top and bottom. Possibly to make it easier to get at lights and wires later, but he gave it a good tug and the side came across from the quarter panel.

Okay, now the fun part.

Gareth returned to his original overhead spot, rather than climbing underneath, like he had planned originally. Quick double-check, but Baker was back and staying out of his way, about fifty meters off to his right.

He took a deep breath. Or whatever a Star Dragon did in deep space where there wasn't any air.

Settled his toes into their holes and grabbed on, foot-fists holding him tightly in place.

Stretch out and over the back of the truck. Grab hold of that panel, right below the door, where the seam had failed earlier.

Pull.

Nothing.

No, unacceptable.

PULL.

Movement. Not much, but proof of concept.

Gareth focused his entire being on that top weld and flexed all the way to the tip of his tail.

It started slowly, failing by millimeters and fighting him for every bit, but it moved. After about three centimeters, something snapped somewhere inside, and the metal began to deform. He pulled more, but the door was warping now as much as it folded. Still, good enough for his purposes.

He let go and flowed around into the opening he had ripped. The back plate gap was about a meter wide, which was enough to get his head, arms, and shoulders inside.

His snout was actually touching the emergency bubble now, and Morty, being Morty, just had to boop him on the snoot with a finger and a laugh that the membrane transmitted.

Gareth rumbled with a laugh, and then set his arms on the floor, using the Elohynn's throne-like chair as an anchor point. He flexed his shoulder and back up and out, growling with the intensity. The metal moved more, failing under the torque Gareth was forcing into it.

It failed with a snap, breaking loose.

Gareth had hold of the chair, so he didn't embarrass himself again, with witnesses this time. Instead, he glanced back and caught the back plate with his left foot, holding it in place, more or less. The throne was in the way, so he found the pins holding it to the deck and snapped them off. He slid it around to the side and stuffed it into the front seat, out of his way and the bubble.

He let go and backed out of the cabin, flowing up and over to the driver's door. His arms weren't long enough in this form, so he pulled open the door and stuck his head in.

Just because Morty had started it, Gareth head-butted the emergency cocoon once, his own boop that picked it up and shoved it softly out into space, now that the entire rear of the vehicle was wide enough for it to get out without catching on anything.

"Baker," Gareth rumbled over the radio. "All yours."

He moved to the top of the truck and snagged the floating panel. After a moment of thought, he stuffed it inside and wedged it well enough to hold. At some point, a tow ship would have to grab the truck and move it to an impound yard. Otherwise, it might fall to earth and maybe have enough metal to survive reentry.

Not good.

Baker was EVA now. Her suit had little jets on the backpack that she used to capture the cocoon, like a sheep dog, and herd them into the open rear door of the truck. The door closed and the three were safe.

Under arrest for a variety of crimes and in really deep doo-doo, but safe from death today, and that was all that mattered right now.

"What about you?" Baker asked, turning her jets to face him as she waited outside the airlock for it to cycle.

"When you get back, open a tube and I'll fly through it," Gareth replied.

She was silent for a moment, deep in thought or maybe talking to Grodray on another channel.

"Sun's coming up over Londra," she observed. "You'll be visible."

"You would never be able to keep something like this secret now anyway," Gareth retorted. "Might as well make a splash."

More silence.

"You sure about this, Gareth?"

He heard Grodray's voice on the line this time. Senior Constable Jackeith Grodray who was secretly a Prime Investigator. A Level-7 instead of a Level-4. The man in charge, but still keeping a very low profile. And he could hide even better in the shadow of a Star Dragon.

"I am," Gareth rumbled back.

"Very good," Grodray said. "Stand by."

A golden portal opened in front of the rescue truck, and the vehicle moved carefully into it, disappearing like a soap bubble on a sunny day.

Gareth waited.

"Okay, Gareth," Baker said. "We're clear of the landing point and moving away. You have a clear flight path."

"Thank you," he said.

The golden tube in front of him represented all the weirdness that had upended his life over the last two months. Perhaps it was appropriate that it would open the next phase in his cursed, or perhaps charmed existence.

The underworld had been rife with unbelievable tales of a giant, flying lizard hunting bad guys. Nobody would doubt them after this.

And he was also a good guy, rescuing people from certain death.

That legend would take shape as well.

For the briefest, scariest moment, Gareth wondered if his appearance might trigger some bizarre new religion. None of the known species could become a dragon, and nobody would know the truth except a very few on both sides of the law.

Would people think he was one of the Chaa, returned to the *Accord of Souls* to help fight evil? Would they worship him?

He was sad that Pastor Jacob wasn't here to advise him, but the man had helped shape him along the way. Gareth would do what was right.

Whatever the cost.

He turned to the golden portal and began to flap, building up speed.

There was a flash of light, over almost before it began, and he was suddenly at gravity's mercy again.

Down became down, and the morning air had turned so cool that his breath steamed when he let go and drew a new breath into his lungs.

The sun was just above the horizon over Londra, painting the cotton-candy sky almost the same reds as that painting he had experienced last night. She hadn't been painting the sunset, that Grace woman.

She had been facing the dawn. The new beginning.

Hope.

Gareth let loose a cry of pure joy as he banked over and began to slowly orbit the Hall of Art.

His story was finally beginning.

"I'M CONCERNED about his paper, Loughty," the man said.

Royston held his tongue. The cluttered oak desk between them, stacked with papers and old tomes, might as well have been a battlefield drawn up between two armies. He had expected what was coming, and wasn't about to back down one scintilla on this.

Not even to this man could make him: Dr. Sir Westfield van Duren-Abbott, PhD, FRS, GMU, KCB, GBE.

Fellow of the Royal Society. Past Guardian of the Mathematical Union. Knight Grand Cross, Order of the British Empire. Knight Commander, Order of the Bath. Even the best-selling author of a popular book on the shape of the universe and humanity's place in it.

Sir West was probably the only mathematician alive that the man on the street might recognize by name. Professor Emeritus, King's College, and all that.

Royston smiled grimly at his old mentor and set his teeth to prevent the growl from escaping his mouth. Now was not the time. Even with Sir West's office door closed, this was not the place.

Royston leaned himself into the wingback chair and forced his muscles to relax. The walls on three sides of the oversized office were covered with bookshelves, and at least four of his books were in here somewhere, along with all twenty-three of Sir West's.

When the man realized that Royston wasn't going to rise to the bait, Sir West sighed.

The man looked every one of his eighty-three years, with a wild fringe of white hair surrounding a sea of liver spots on the bald top. Even his tweeds might be older than Royston. The eyes were hazel most of the time, and gave utter lie to the rest of the man's unkempt appearance as a fussy old duffer headed down to the pub for a pint.

Sir West had lost barely any of the genius that put him at the top of the field sixty years ago and kept him there.

"Yes, concerned that you've gone about this all wrong, Loughty," the man repeated himself.

"Why is that, Sir West?" Royston finally asked.

If they were going to have to play this game, he was going to make the old man work for it. Simple as that.

"Your co-author, Roy," Sir West intoned in a severe, almost condescending voice.

"Oh?" Royston fired back innocently.

As if he hadn't woken up this morning and spent his breakfast and the flight down here to England preparing for this battle.

"I appreciate that she is your daughter," Sir West equivocated. "And a very sharp girl, but this paper has the potential to utterly destroy your reputation, Loughty. I wouldn't want hers to suffer any collateral damage."

"What's wrong with the contents of the paper, Sir West?" Royston challenged, letting just the thinnest edge of his pique show through.

The man had been his mentor for nearly three decades now. Challenging his genius was like arguing with God himself about things.

"You claim to have invented an entirely new mathematics, Loughty," the older man was exasperated. "As if your place in history is to rival Newton and Leibniz. Higher dimensions of space? Wormholes? Ye gads, man, that's the fanciful conjecture of the worst speculative fiction writers. Newton was surpassed by Einstein, but nobody in the last five hundred years has been able to prove the German wrong. And everyone has tried."

"I'm aware of that, Sir West," Royston replied with a sniff.

"This paper will get you laughed out of the Royal Society, Loughty," Sir West pleaded. "Burn it, before anybody else finds out, and I swear I will never mention it again."

"I've already begun designing the first generator, Sir West," Royston replied.

"You've what?"

"The theory supports a certain type of radiation, previously unknown anywhere in any proposed model of physics, being a residue from such a device as an electromagnetic signature," Royston said.

"So?" the man shifted uncomfortably in his chair.

"I've seen that radiation," Royston replied, eyes squinting with fury. "Detected it under circumstances that were utterly impossible to explain. If the security clearance around the incident wasn't so high, I could tell you about it. Instead I might suggest you ask the Queen when you next have lunch with her. Perhaps a tour of The Arsenal and a look at the bleeding edge of research might be in order, sometime soon."

He left it at that. That was exactly as much hint as he could offer without getting himself in trouble, but Sir Westfield van Duren-Abbott was a bright enough fellow to understand the clues and follow the breadcrumbs to enlightenment.

If he really wanted to know the truth.

"And this?" he gestured at the folder between them on the desk.

The paper was amazingly thin, as those things went. More than half of it was an Appendix filled with the new vocabulary of terms and symbols Royston had been forced to invent, to try to explore the ideas that took shape under the influence of that young lady's rock and roll.

The paper itself was an exploration of several higher orders of dimensionality, arranged like layers in a puff pastry and separated by walls of radiation that might be some bizarre, previously-unsuspected residue of the Big Bang itself.

That awaited a future paper to explore. And possibly entire generations of science fiction writers to prove right. He looked forward to dropping a small and rather polite bomb on the Royal Society sometime soon. Possibly by opening a wormhole across the length of a desk and rolling a marble through it. That demonstration might require an entire atomic pile to power it, but the expressions of shock on those old fart's faces would be worth every pfennig.

"How would you classify this?" the older scientist pressed.

"A roadmap to the future, old man," Royston snapped. "I don't know what's out there, or who, but I have strong suggestions that we'll find someone when we get there. The rest is just the work of some extremely competent and creative mechanical engineers. I have a number of those on call, up in orbit."

"So you're going to go through with it?" Sir West demanded abrasively.

"Indeed," Royston smiled. He leaned back again, when he realized he had leaned forward far enough to put his hands on the desk again.

"And you will share credit with a woman?" Sir West's voice got ugly.

"Did you know that King's College used to admit women into their doctoral programs, Sir West?" Royston purred icily. "That many schools did, back in the old days before Earth Force? Back at the dawn of the Space Age?"

"And next I suppose you'll tell me that the Etruscans were a co-equal society. And the Vikings and so many others. Ancient history, and she has nothing more than a basic degree."

"Truth," Royston acknowledged. "And since no admissions council would grant her leave to attend, she has instead been my principal assistant for several years, when she might have been successfully pursuing such advanced degrees. After me, she's the only other expert on the topic. If people intend to be snotty enough to me on the matter, I might send her to make all my presentations and remain in my lab in orbit."

That got the man's attention. Royston could see Sir West envisioning a woman standing before the Royal Society, dressed in that red skirt and tunic, representing Sky Patrol. They had admitted women once, as well. In the so-called Dark Ages of Technology.

Royston smiled at the possibility of her on the talk shows, describing the work as an equal partner, and not just the daughter of the inventor.

Sir West leaned back in turn, cooling his ardor by force of will. He could see the precipice that Royston had walked him to, like a bear trap hidden in the low grass.

"Let me make a few inquiries," he half-promised, suddenly understanding the lever Royston held.

Archimedes had warned these bastards, but not enough of them had listened.

"How soon until you build a device?" Sir West asked carefully.

"This one will exceed my current budget," Royston replied. "I'll be sending this paper up the chain at Sky Patrol, requesting additional funds and assistance. They have a powerful, vested interest in the topic that I am not at liberty to discuss, currently."

"Would you consider building it at King's College?" Sir West asked, dancing expertly around the topic.

"When the Sky Marshal asks me to present my theories to the Secretary, it might be helpful if Her Majesty was willing to chat with the Chancellor on the topic," Royston allowed.

The Americans would also be quite interested, and willing to throw money at him. And they dominated both Earth Force in general and Sky Force in particular.

Very interested.

Because someone had kidnapped Gareth St. John Dankworth.

The Americans would want to have a friendly chat with those folks.

At least it would start friendly. Americans were like that.

"I shall make some inquiries, Loughty," Sir West finally temporized. "Will this really potentially give us the galaxy?"

"That is my hope, Sir West," Royston replied. "That is my goal."

WITNESS

CONSTABLE BAKER SMILED as the six people were marched onto the low stage and lined up under extremely bright lights. She was on the other side of a thick window, sitting in darkness with a pair of Yuudixtl men who were practically vibrating with excitement, in spite of the handcuffs around their wrists.

This was all just a formality anyway. Six Elohynn were lined up. Two of them slouched in the uniform of the Constabulary. One of those and another were female. Another was a well-known, local sports reporter with a sense of humor. One was a random stranger off the street, willing to take an hour off and get lunch in the deal.

And one fat, old man Elohynn that had been utterly bullet-proof until yesterday.

She smiled some more, letting it spread so far across her face that she was afraid she might start to glow.

"Number four," the neared Yuudixtl crowed.

She had only met Morty in the flesh a few hours ago, but she had been reading reports and hearing stories from both Dankworth and Liamssen about the lizardman for nearly two months now. He was just as silly, as sarcastic, and as sharp as they had warned her.

Eveth picked up a microphone and spoke into it.

"Number four, step forward," she commanded.

It helped that he was the only one wearing cuffs in there, but this was just a formality.

Omerlon took an angry step forward. He looked like he wanted to punch the glass, had his hands been in front. Perhaps he might head-butt it yet.

"That's him," the other one said.

Xiomber. Supposedly egg-brother to Morty. Partners in crime and mischief. And willing to spend the last three hours, on tape, detailing every crime they could remember, with names, dates, places, and amounts. And not just Sarzynski's gang, as these two had spent twenty years being bad guys for a number of outfits.

It would take her weeks, and maybe months to suck these two dry. And they seemed even more excited at the prospect than she did.

Bizarre.

"Morty?" she asked.

"Correct," Morty said. "Number four."

"The rest of you may go," she said into the mic. "Thank you for your service."

"You bastards got nothing on me," Omerlon snarled.

"On the contrary, Omerlon," Baker said with an infectious smile that the other two seemed to have picked up. "I have you on four counts of attempted murder, including attempted murder of a Constabulary Officer."

Three of the folks in the line-up had departed. The two Elohynn officers were pushing Omerlon the other direction, towards the holding cells.

"May I?" Morty hopped off his stool and approached with a hand out.

Baker shrugged and handed him the microphone.

"Hey, Omerlon," Morty cat-called the Elohynn crime boss. "You were right. See you in hell."

He handed her back the mic and moved towards the two officers at the back of the room, almost skipping with glee.

She had no idea what was going on, but this was going to be fun.

Because Omerlon? Yeah, he was about to enter hell.

HOME

GARETH ENTERED the research lab as quietly as he could. Talyarkinash was working on a screen with her profile towards him, tracing something on the screen with a nail painted green today. It looked like his silhouette on the screen, so she was probably calculating new options.

He cleared his throat as he got closer.

Talyarkinash turned and blinked in surprise. She took three steps across the lab and engulfed him in a hug, as short as she was.

"You did it," she said. "I saw you on the morning news. It was glorious. You were glorious."

Gareth untangled himself a little and leaned back enough to smile at her.

"You did it," he said. "I was able to rescue Morty and Xiomber in that truck, along with another man, by having Baker bounce me to orbit. I could have never done anything like that without your help."

"Morty? Xiomber" she cried with joy. "You found them?"

"And arrested them," Gareth said. "They're in custody downstairs while Baker and Grodray work out what to do with them."

"What will happen?" she asked, leaning back herself until they only touched where hands contacted ribs.

"There is a precedence," he grinned slyly. "Ex-criminals willing to turn state's evidence and work with the Constabulary."

"Like you?" she teased.

Gareth's grin turned into a smile. Technically, he was an illegal alien, illegally upgraded. And trying to do good.

"I might know others," he teased back. "Have you had breakfast? I've been using the Star Dragon form for hours and I'm famished. Plus, I want to talk to you about some things. I had a lot of time up in space alone, since the others were trapped in an emergency cocoon. They could wave, but I had nobody to talk to except Baker and Grodray."

She stepped back and turned to her workstation, hitting a button to save everything and power it down for now.

"I would love to join you for breakfast, Gareth," she said. "What did you need?"

"On the one hand, I have a few questions about maybe upgrading the Star Dragon," he replied. "Or maybe creating a second, larger form I could shift into when I needed to go beyond the normal for size and strength."

"Okay," she said, moving towards the door and opening it. "That's actually along the lines of what I have been working on up until now. What was the second part?"

"How will the average person react to seeing me as a dragon?" Gareth asked. "I will become a symbol of fear to the criminals, which was what I intended, but will the rest of the *Accord of Souls* see me as one of the Chaa returned? Will they think I'm a god?"

"Oh, Gareth," she leaned close and placed a palm on the chest of his grinder wool blazer. "That's not something I can help you with. You'll need a priest, or maybe a philosopher."

"No," Gareth corrected her. "What I need is a friend."

READ MORE!

Be sure to read all of the Star Dragon books!

Birth of the Star Dragon
Flight of the Star Dragon
Call of the Star Dragon
Shadow of the Star Dragon
Trial of the Star Dragon

ABOUT THE AUTHOR

Blaze Ward writes science fiction in the Alexandria Station universe (Jessica Keller, The Science Officer, The Story Road, etc.) as well as several other science fiction universes, such as Star Dragon, the Collective, and more. He also writes odd bits of high fantasy with swords and orcs. In addition, he is the Editor and Publisher of *Boundary Shock Quarterly Magazine*. You can find out more at his website www.blazeward.com, as well as Facebook, Goodreads, and other places.

Blaze's works are available as ebooks, paper, and audio, and can be found at a variety of online vendors. His newsletter comes out quarterly, and you can also follow his blog on his website. He really enjoys interacting with fans, and looks forward to any and all questions—even ones about his books!

Never miss a release!
If you'd like to be notified of new releases, sign up for my newsletter.

I will never spam you or use your email for nefarious purposes. You can also unsubscribe at any time.

http://www.blazeward.com/newsletter/

Connect with Blaze!

Web: www.blazeward.com
Boundary Shock Quarterly (BSQ):
https://www.boundaryshockquarterly.com/

facebook.com/KRPBlaze

goodreads.com/Blaze_Ward

ABOUT KNOTTED ROAD PRESS

Knotted Road Press fiction specializes in dynamic writing set in mysterious, exotic locations.

Knotted Road Press non-fiction publishes autobiographies, business books, cookbooks, and how-to books with unique voices.

Knotted Road Press creates DRM-free ebooks as well as high-quality print books for readers around the world.

With authors in a variety of genres including literary, poetry, mystery, fantasy, and science fiction, Knotted Road Press has something for everyone.

Knotted Road Press
www.KnottedRoadPress.com